Books by Liz Harris
in the Linford Romance Library:

A DANGEROUS HEART

A WESTERN HEART

Wyoming, 1880: Childhood sweethearts Rose McKinley and Will Hyde have always been destined to marry; and with their parents just as keen on the match, there is nothing to stop them. Except perhaps Cora, Rose's younger sister. Lovesick and hung up on Will, she is fed up with the happy couple. So when the handsome Mr Galloway comes to town and turns Rose's head, Cora sees an opportunity to get what she wants: Will . . .

LIZ HARRIS

◆

A WESTERN HEART

Complete and Unabridged

LINFORD
Leicester

First published in Great Britain in 2014 by
Choc Lit Limited
Surrey

First Linford Edition
published 2018
by arrangement with
Choc Lit Limited
Surrey

A catalogue record for this book is available
from the British Library.

ISBN 978–1–4448–3685–1

Published by
F. A. Thorpe (Publishing)
Anstey, Leicestershire

Set by Words & Graphics Ltd.
Anstey, Leicestershire
Printed and bound in Great Britain by
T. J. International Ltd., Padstow, Cornwall

This book is printed on acid-free paper

1

Wyoming Territory
Early in June, 1880

'Not again.' Rose McKinley breathed inwardly as she put the last of the hoecakes on to the plate.

She pulled off her apron, hastily excused herself to her mother and half ran from the kitchen into the hall. It was almost more than she could bear, she thought, as she hurried along the passageway in a rustle of pink and white gingham, having to endure her ma's continual hinting that it was time she and Will announced their engagement. It was about the only thing her folks seemed able to talk about, and Will's folks were just as bad.

She'd started helping her mother and Maria with the cooking just after breakfast, and almost as soon as they'd

1

begun, her ma had started on about her and Will. She'd put up with it for as long as her help had been needed, but she'd reached the point where she knew she'd scream if she heard another word on the subject.

It wouldn't have been as bad if Cora had been helping in the kitchen with her, she thought as she reached the front door, but Cora hadn't been there — she was still at the Hydes' ranch, where she'd been staying overnight with Will's sister, Mattie, and she wouldn't be back till early that evening.

Her sister could be really irritating at times, but when it came to Will and the wedding she'd been surprisingly helpful. Being only two years younger, she was old enough to see how uncomfortable Rose had begun to feel with all the engagement hints, and to Rose's relief and gratitude, Cora had started to change the subject as soon as anyone mentioned Will and marriage.

But with Cora away, there'd been no one to move her ma on to a different topic, and she'd had enough.

She flung the door open and went out on to the wooden veranda that ran round the house. Pausing a moment, she drew a deep breath and stared across the dusty wide yard to the sprawling acres of green grass and yellow sagebrush that lay beyond the outer fence, stretching out to the low rolling hills.

On either side of the dirt track that snaked away from the ranch — a wide brown swathe cutting through the seemingly endless grassland — cows were grazing, dark dots interspersed with larger patches of brown where several of the cows had bunched together around clumps of the better grass.

Feeling calmer, she went slowly over to the veranda railing and leaned against it, squinting slightly in the bright light of the mid-morning sun as she gazed towards the distant blue horizon.

She loved Will and she knew that he loved her. He'd been her closest friend for as long as she could remember and although they'd never talked about it in

3

so many words, they'd always known that one day they'd marry. And one day they would, she was sure. But it would be when it suited her and Will to do so, not their folks.

Not that she blamed their parents for being in a hurry to see them wed. Her pa had built McKinley Ranch into one of the most successful in their part of Wyoming Territory, and Will's pa had done the same with the neighbouring Hyde Ranch. With Will being an only son, he'd one day run Hyde Ranch, and with her being the older daughter on a ranch without a son, the two ranches would be linked from the moment they wed. From that time on, the Hydes and McKinleys would work closely together until the day came that they united and became one of the largest spreads in the Territory.

She wasn't stupid — she could see all the advantages of a marriage between her and Will, just as their folks could. But they should be allowed to do things at their own pace, not at anyone else's.

Footsteps sounded loud on the hard wood floor of the hall. Rose straightened up. In a moment, her ma would come out on to the veranda and ask her to go back inside and continue helping with the cooking. And as soon as she was back in the kitchen, the hints about Will would start again.

Well, she'd already had more than enough of that subject, and she wasn't going to wait around for any more.

She gathered up her skirts, ran down the veranda steps and hurried across the yard in the direction of the horses' barn. She'd take the buggy and go and find Will. She knew he'd be somewhere near his house as he'd told her they were going to be branding the last of the late calves that morning. If she left at once, she'd be there just in time to join the Hydes for lunch.

As she neared the barn, she saw the ranch foreman coming out of the tackle shed next to it.

'Jesse!' she called to him. 'I was hoping to find you here. Will you hitch the horses up? I'm going to Hyde Ranch, and I'm taking the buggy so I can bring Cora back with me. If Ma comes looking for me, will you tell her where I've gone?' Behind her, she heard her mother call out her name, and she quickened her pace.

'Don't tell her for a bit, though, Jesse,' she added. 'I'll wait in the barn till the buggy's ready.'

'Sure thing, Miz Rose. I'll get the harness right now,' Jesse said.

As she stepped into the barn, she glanced to her right and glimpsed the broad grin on Jesse's face as he turned into the shed.

★   ★   ★

An hour later, Rose pulled up the buggy next to a long metal trough of water at the side of the Hyde ranch house, jumped down and glanced across the yard at a couple of ranch hands who were busy removing bobsled runners from the wagons that had been used for travel in the snow.

One of the men looked up in her direction, and she promptly waved at him and indicated that the horses needed to be unhitched from the buggy. He said something to the man working with him, then dropped his tools to the ground and started towards her.

She quickly wound the reins over the hitching rail, waved her thanks to the approaching ranch hand and began to make her way past the front of the ranch house, brushing down her skirt as she headed in the direction of the west barn and the corrals that lay behind it. The distant sounds coming from beyond the barn told her that that was where she'd find the ranch hands, and Will was more than likely to be where they were.

As she drew near to West Barn, the pungent smell of cow dung hit her. The piles of soiled straw and dung heaped up outside the barn told that it was being cleaned, and she went up to the open entrance and peered into the dark interior.

'Will?' she called, her voice echoing beneath the high wooden roof.

A man came out of the front stall, a pitchfork in his hand. 'He ain't here, ma'am,' he told her. 'He's out brandin' with the ropers. I reckon you'll find 'em all in the far corral.'

Nodding to him, she went back to the track and made her way quickly past an empty wagon standing alongside West Barn. Her steps slowed as the corrals came into sight. All appeared to be empty except for the furthest one. Standing still, she raised herself on the tips of her boots and stared ahead at the far corral.

Will was the first person she saw. His brown felt hat low over his face, he sat easy in the saddle as he and three or four ropers urged their horses among the jostling cattle. From the way they were moving, it looked as if they were about to begin the branding. Disappointed, she realised it was too late to let him know she was there — she'd have to wait till they'd finished.

She glanced back at the barn and the empty wagon. The wagon was in the shade and she'd have a better view if she sat on it. She went quickly back to it and climbed up. A cloud of buffalo gnats swarmed in the air around her as she settled, and she impatiently swatted them away. Leaning forwards, she fixed her eyes firmly on Will.

Riding high among the cowmen on his chestnut mare, Boy, he had one hand lightly on the reins, the other at his side, a ring of coiled rawhide hanging from his fingers. It was impossible for her see his face, though, as he'd pulled down the brim of his hat so as to shield his eyes from the glare of the late morning sun.

She looked at the coil of leather in his hand. So he was going to act as a roper that morning, she thought in amusement, and she smiled to herself. He never missed a chance of joining in with the work on the ranch. He might be slow in asking her to marry him, but there wasn't any part of ranch work that he didn't throw himself into without a moment's hesitation.

A sudden shriek of girlish laughter sounded above the urgent lowing of the cattle and the barking of the round-up dog which would be darting in and out between the legs of the cows and their calves. She looked quickly to the right of the corral and saw that Cora and Mattie were sitting atop the wooden fence, their eyes on Will and the cowmen.

She sat up in amazement.

Cora had told her that she and Mattie would be trimming their dresses and lining their bonnets for the annual picnic in Hope the following day. It was why her sister had wanted to stay over, despite the fact there was cooking to be done at home for the picnic. And it wasn't just for the picnic — they had a special guest for dinner that night. He was going to be arriving that evening and staying a few days while he discussed business matters with their pa.

Either they'd finished their dresses more quickly than they'd expected or they'd changed their minds about improving them. But even if either of those things was the case, they'd never liked watching the calves being done and they'd always avoided it in the past. So why had they chosen to come outside on what was going to be a branding morning?

She stared at them, puzzled.

Cora's eyes were following Will's every movement while Mattie's were fixed on the cowmen.

Her gaze moved from Cora to Will, and back again to Cora. She saw her sister break out into laughter at something Will had called across to her. She looked quickly back at Will — he'd pushed up the brim of his Stetson and was wiping his forehead with the back of his hand. She could see him grinning across at Cora.

Her heart missed a beat.

She looked back at Mattie. The girl's eyes were on the cowman approaching

11

her, his thumbs tucked into the belt of his denims, a swagger in his walk. He must be the new ranch hand, she thought. She couldn't see him clearly, but she was pretty sure she didn't recognise him. He stopped at the foot of the fence, looked up at Mattie and spoke to her. Blushing with visible pleasure, Mattie glanced down at him and giggled.

So it wasn't the branding that had drawn them to the corral. It was obvious Mattie had wanted to see the new cowman but wouldn't have been able to go and watch him by herself.

She felt sharp irritation with the two girls. Mattie should know that even with Cora at her side, it wasn't seemly to sit with the men in the way they were, not even if one of them *was* Mattie's brother. And Cora should know that, too.

It wouldn't occur to Will that the girls shouldn't be there — he'd see only their admiration of his skill with the rope — but the girls were both seventeen now, and that was plenty old enough for them to know how a lady should behave. Their folks would be real mad if they knew the two of them were hanging around the cowmen like they were.

The cry 'Hot iron!' cut through her thoughts.

She glanced at the field to the left of the corral. Beyond the fence, a thin wisp of smoke curled into the air. A cowman standing by the plume of smoke was waving at Will, obviously telling him the iron was hot enough for them to begin. She looked back at Will. He'd raised his hand in acknowledgement, and was turning his horse to face the calves in the corral.

Her elbows on her knees, she watched him choose his calf and line up his horse. The rope in his hand, he raised his arm and swung the rope high in the air above him, circling it with a confident fluid grace, his forearm gleaming gold in the light of the morning sun. Then with a sudden surge of power, he swung his body forward in line with the rope and sent a loop flying through the air and over the head of the calf.

The new young ranch hand shouted something to him. Laughing, Will jerked the slack in his rein and pulled the rope taut around the calf's neck. Bracing his weight in his stirrups to hold firm in the saddle against the thrusts of the calf, he turned his horse and started to drag the calf out of the corral, half-hidden from her by the cloud of dust thrown up by the struggling animal and the hoofs of his horse.

Her eyes followed him as he rode out of the corral, one hand lightly holding the reins and saddle horn, and the other gripping the rope attached to the calf behind him. One of the ropers cantered out of the corral after him. He, too, was carrying a loop of rawhide in his hand. To her great irritation, the mounted roper blocked her view of Will. She moved further along the wagon seat, but still couldn't get a better view of him than from where she'd originally been sitting. Abandoning the attempt, she turned her attention back to Cora and Mattie.

They were no longer sitting on the fence, but had wandered across to the entrance of the corral. Mattie had stopped just short of the entrance and was talking to the new ranch hand. Cora was standing a few steps further on, leaning against the wooden fence, staring out at the pasture in the direction of Will.

She stood up and stared intently at Cora.

She could see Will better now, too. The roper following him, he was riding back to the corral, his right arm stretched out behind him as he pulled the calf along.

As he approached the entrance to the corral, Cora took a step back to give him more room to go through, turning as she did so to gaze after him. There was a broad smile on her face as she watched him ride into the centre of the corral, hold his horse firm, and wait while one of the men shook the rope from the calf's neck so that it could run back to its mother. The calf released, he swung his horse to face Cora, and Rose saw her sister's smile widen.

Laughing, Mattie ran forward, gave Cora a playful push in Will's direction, and then went swiftly back to the new ranch hand.

Throwing a quick glance in Mattie's direction, Cora smoothed down her overskirt and walked over to Will.

Rose's heart gave an anxious leap.

She hastily climbed down from the wagon and hurried across to the far corral, wiping the dust from the rear of her skirt as she walked. She reached the entrance, nodded at the nearby ropers and then paused. Standing just inside the fence, she stared at Will and Cora.

Will was looking down at Cora. She was standing next to his horse, her back to Rose, stroking the horse's nose. Although Rose couldn't see her face, from the angle and movement of Cora's head, she could tell that Cora was saying something to Will. His eyes being shaded by his hat, she couldn't see the expression in them, but as he started to move his horse away to join the ropers, she saw clearly enough the warmth in the smile he gave her sister.

As a nameless fear crept through her, coiling its icy hand around her heart, Rose began to walk towards them.

2

As Cora turned away from Will, she caught sight of Rose. She stopped abruptly and stared at her sister, scowling.

'What are you doing here?' she asked, annoyance sharpening her voice.

Will twisted towards Rose in his saddle, and his face broke out into a smile of pleasure.

'Rose!' he exclaimed. 'I didn't expect to see you today.'

He swung his six-foot frame off the horse, let the reins fall to the ground and walked over to her, rubbing his hands on the sides of his denims. His sweat-slicked shirt clung to his lean chest, outlining the muscles that rippled with his every step. Reaching her, he pulled off his hat and ran his fingers through his sun-streaked brown hair. The smell of rawhide, horse and sweat enveloped her.

'I thought I'd surprise you,' she said lightly, moving closer to him.

'You sure did that!' he said with a delighted grin. 'But that don't mean I'm not pleased to see you, 'cos I sure am.'

'I should hope so.' Rose laughed. She heard the tinge of nervousness in her own voice, and bit her lower lip as she looked up at him.

Open affection shone from the depths of the clear blue eyes that smiled back at her, and the shapeless anxiety that had been welling up in her body drained away. Relief washed through her and she beamed up at him.

'I'm guessin' you've come to help us with the branding,' he said, a note of amusement in his voice. 'I sure am sorry, Rose, but you're too late — we've just done the last of the calves.'

'Aw, shucks,' she said, pouting in exaggerated disappointment. 'Then I reckon I'll have to find some other way of amusing myself.'

'I might just be able to help out with

that.' He grinned at her, slapped his dust-covered Stetson against his thigh and put it back on. 'We're gonna be mucking out the horse barn this afternoon. The Big Circle horses will be arrivin' Monday and we're gettin' ready for them. They can cover twenty miles of country in a half a day, and on a ranch with the acreage of ours, that'll be a big saving in time when it comes to gatherin' in the cattle so we're keen to settle them in as soon as possible. Maybe helpin' us with the mucking out is the sorta thing that'd amuse you. What d'you reckon?'

She laughed, reached up to him and pulled the brim of his hat down over his eyes. 'What I reckon is, we've got different ideas of havin' fun, Will Hyde.'

'I asked what you were doin' here?' Cora repeated, coming up to them, her hands on her hips, her green eyes flashing angrily. From her position behind Cora, Mattie glared at Rose.

'Why, I've come to collect you, Cora,' Rose said, glancing at her sister. 'I thought I'd save the Hydes the trouble of bringing you back home. And as you've obviously finished trimming your dresses or you wouldn't be out here, and as we've just heard how busy they're gonna be this afternoon, I reckon that was a good decision.'

'Cora can stay for lunch, though, can't she, Will?' Mattie pleaded. 'Ma's expectin' her.'

Cora looked hopefully at Will. 'Mattie's right — your ma invited me. We've got plans for after lunch so I was gonna go home later this afternoon. Ma said I could stay till this evening so long as I was back in time for dinner with the visitor, and it's up to my ma what I do, not Rose. I know you heard her say that, Rose, so you shouldn't've come so early.'

Rose gave a slight shrug of her shoulders. 'I must've forgotten. Anyway, apart from wanting to stop anyone from having to harness the horses to bring you home, Cora, I kinda thought I'd like to see Will.' She turned back to Will and glanced up at him from beneath long dark eyelashes. 'Feeling that way, I got into the buggy on an impulse and came.'

He shook his head in mock admiration. 'That was a mighty fine impulse, Rose. And of course, it wasn't a way of putting some distance between you and the cooking this morning.' The corners of his eyes crinkled in amusement as he looked down at her. 'I seem to recall Cora telling me you were gonna be helping your ma today.'

She threw back her head and laughed. 'You know me too well. Although actually you're wrong. I have been helping Ma all morning, and by the time I left to come here, most of the cooking had been done and I wasn't needed real bad any longer.'

'Is that so?' he said with a smile. 'Then let's put my knowledge of you to the test, shall we? Right now, I reckon you're hoping we're all gonna walk over to the house and tell Ma that you'll be stayin' to lunch as well as Cora.'

'I guess you do know me,' she said, a lilt in her voice.

'And you know she'll say 'yup' and be mighty pleased to see you at our table.'

She glanced at him. Their eyes met and they smiled at each other.

Then she turned to her sister. 'I hope it's okay with you if I join you for lunch, Cora.'

'I guess,' Cora said, her voice sulky.

Rose went to her sister and put her arm around her shoulders. 'I'm sorry if you think I've ruined your day. I sure didn't mean to.'

'But you did, anyway,' Cora snapped, and she shrugged off Rose's arm and moved closer to Mattie.

'Why don't you take Cora and Rose up to the house, Mattie?' Will said, glancing at the faces of the two sisters. 'As soon as we've finished sending the cows and calves out to graze again, I'll wash up for lunch and join you.'

★ ★ ★

The late afternoon sun was hanging low on the horizon when the ranch came into sight.

'D'you intend to speak to me at all for the rest of today?' Rose asked, slowing down the buggy as she guided it beneath a high wooden crossbeam burned with the words *McKinley Ranch*. 'You didn't say a word to me all through lunch, and you've been silent for the whole of the journey back.'

There was no reply from Cora.

Rose glanced across at her: Cora's arms were folded, and her face was closed as she stared fixedly ahead.

She turned her attention back to the track and carried on without speaking until they'd driven past the ranch house to the outbuildings to the right of the family home. Bringing the buggy to halt in front of the horses' shed, Rose climbed down.

Cora didn't move.

'I don't know what's got into you, Cora,' Rose said, her hands still on the reins as she stared up at her sister. 'I wanted to see Will. You're seventeen and old enough to understand that, so I sure don't know why you're so angry with me.'

'It's always about you, isn't it? It's never about what I want,' Cora snapped, glaring down at Rose. 'You suddenly decide you wanna see Will, so off you go to the Hydes, and that means my day with Mattie's ruined. What I want matters, too, you know.'

'I know it does, and I've already told you I'm sorry I spoilt your day. You're right, I didn't think. But to be fair, we stayed on after lunch and in the end you've only lost about an hour — you'd have had to be back for dinner this evening as we've got that guest coming.'

Cora glared at her. 'If you say so.'

'Also, both of us coming home a mite early could be useful for Ma,' Rose went on. 'There might be something left we could do to help. So I'm not the only one thinking of herself. You're not exactly thinkin' of Ma, are you?'

'You can twist anything,' Cora

muttered. Her face sullen, she climbed down from the buggy. 'I'll find a wrangler to deal with the horses. You can do what you want.' She spun round, ducked under the hitching rail and went into the horses' barn, calling for Jesse.

Dropping the reins, Rose walked slowly across the wide yard to the main house. As she stepped through the doorway into the hall, she heard the sound of Cora running up behind her.

Turning round, she paused to let Cora catch her up.

'Because you're older, you always take over, Rose,' Cora said, obviously still annoyed with her sister. 'You may not know you do it, but you do. All through lunch, it was you that Will and his folks were talking to. And it was you doing all the talking when we sat on the veranda after lunch. No one remembered Mattie and I were there. And it's the same here — it's always you, never me.'

Rose gestured her helplessness. 'But

you know why that is. It's not just Ma and Pa — it's the Hydes, too. They all want to see our two ranches united. It's not about me: it's about horses, cows, land, buildings. But you know that — why, you've even begun to help me out by changing the subject whenever they start on weddings.'

'Then maybe you should think about helping me out sometimes. Maybe you could see that I'm not left out of the conversation. Mattie, too. We're not babies, you know.'

'Okay. I guess that's fair. But you've got to make an effort, too, Cora. You're a quiet person — except when you're angry with me, of course,' she added with a wry smile. 'You don't always speak out enough, and while that's not a bad thing in a lady, it might be well if you made a bigger attempt to join in with conversation. I know you've got a strong mind and you're a real deter- mined person. Maybe you should let folks around here see what's inside you, too. If they did, they'd wanna hear what you'd got to say.'

Cora shrugged her shoulders. 'It's easy for you to say I should join in more. You always know what to say. I don't.'

'You had no problem talkin' to Will this morning, I noticed,' Rose retorted.

'That's 'cos I've known him for years. Not known him as well as you, of course, but I've seen him a lot. He's been around all the time I've been growin' up. Not that he's ever noticed I'm there,' she added.

'From where I was standing, he sure was noticing you today. You both seemed to be doing a lot of laughing with each other. What were you talkin' about that was making you laugh so much?'

Cora opened her mouth to reply.

'Ah, there you are, girls. I thought I heard you,' Julia McKinley said, hurrying from the kitchen into the hall and wiping her hands on her apron. 'It's just as well you're back in good time for dinner — Mr Galloway's gotten here sooner than we expected. I haven't quite finished the preparations for tomorrow's picnic so it'd help me some if one of you sits with your pa and Mr Galloway, and the other helps Maria and me finish up in the kitchen.'

'I'll help you, Ma,' Rose volunteered. 'Cora can sit with Pa and Mr Galloway.'

The two girls exchanged glances. Cora gave her sister a slight smile. Rose giggled.

Julia nodded. 'That's fair enough, Rose. You did rush off rather suddenly this morning,' she said, her voice a trifle sharp. 'With three of us working hard, it won't take long to do what's left. You'll find the men in the living area, Cora. But go up and tidy yourself first.'

She gave them a quick smile, turned and went back to the kitchen. A moment later, they heard the faint sound of her talking to Maria.

'I hope Pa's guest isn't too old and dull,' Cora said, pulling a face. 'The last time someone was referred to Pa by one of his ranching connections, he was so deaf we had to scream everything at him. And Ma and Pa had to shout out every word, too. My throat was so sore after he left that all I could eat for a week was alum.'

She pulled an expression of distaste. They both giggled.

'I guess I'd better go and change,' Cora said, 'and then join Pa and his visitor. Don't be too long, will you? I know I said you'd done more than your share of the talking today. Forget that. I'll be real happy if you come on down as soon as you can and take over from me. I've got a feeling we've a long, dull evening ahead of us.'

★ ★ ★

Holding her skirts and petticoats up, Rose ran down the stairs and then turned to go into the large living area on the right.

As she entered the room, she saw that her father and the visitor were sitting side by side in two of the deep brown leather armchairs, their backs to her. Cora was sitting opposite them on the other side of the low dark wood table.

At least, he didn't have grey hair, and there weren't any unruly whiskers bushing visibly out of the sides of his face, she thought as she stared at the back of the visitor's head.

'Ah, there you are, girl,' Thomas McKinley said, turning slightly in his chair and catching sight of her. He stood up. 'Meet my daughter, Rose, Galloway.'

His back to her, the visitor rose to his feet. Her mouth started to curve into her customary smile of welcome.

He turned to face her, and she stopped abruptly mid-smile.

Hooded jet-black eyes burnt into her with an intensity she wasn't used to, then swept down the length of her body.

She felt herself go red.

Putting her hand to her cheek to cool herself down, she stared at the man.

He was a mighty fine-looking man, she thought. He appeared to be several years older than Will. Like Will, he was tall and lean, but whereas Will's skin was the colour of liquid gold and his eyes as blue as the midday sky, the visitor's skin was only lightly sun-browned. And whereas Will's brown hair had been streaked fair by the sun, the visitor's hair was as dark as his heavy-lidded eyes. Whatever the stranger's business, he certainly wasn't out on the range every day in all weathers.

And whatever his business, he was obviously a successful man. His clothes told her that.

Under a canvas brush jacket, he wore a crisp white shirt tucked into well-cut brown canvas pants that clung to his muscular thighs. His boots were made of the finest quality calf-skin, and the design scored into the polished leather belt that hung low on his hips was hand-tooled. Everything about him shouted out confidence and success. And masculine strength.

'You've two fine-looking daughters, Mr McKinley,' he said glancing from Rose to her father.

Raising her eyes to his profile, she traced the planes and angles of his features, which were highlighted by the reflected glow of the kerosene lamps on the wall and on the table. He turned slightly towards her and caught her looking at him. Their eyes held for a moment, then she turned quickly away.

Her skin tightened around her frame, and she suddenly felt hot and uncomfortable. Swallowing hard, she took a deep breath.

'Rose, I'd like you to meet Nate Galloway. Mr Galloway's gonna be our guest for a few days.' Her father's voice seemed to come from afar.

'Pleased to meet you, Mr Galloway,' she managed to say, her mouth dry.

Nate Galloway stepped forward and took Rose's hand. A jolt ran up her arm, and she made a move to pull her hand away, but his grip was firm. 'And I'm mighty pleased to meet you, ma'am,' he said, his voice a slow drawl. 'Mighty pleased indeed.'

'Go and sit next to your sister, gal,' her pa said, indicating the armchair next to where Cora was sitting.

Nate dropped Rose's hand and stepped back.

Her hand feeling empty, she sat down where her pa had said and pressed her fingers hard against the side of her skirt in an attempt at wiping away the feel of where he'd touched her.

Nate Galloway and Thomas sat down again in the chairs facing her and Cora.

Glancing across the table at her, Nate stretched out his long legs and gave her a lazy smile. She started to blush again, her heart hammering loudly in her chest. Wondering if Cora could hear the thudding, she glanced at her sister.

Her face impassive, Cora was staring at her.

3

'That was a mighty fine meal, Mrs McKinley,' Nate said. 'I appreciate it.'

'I'm real glad you enjoyed it, Mr Galloway,' Julia replied. She glanced at Rose and Cora. 'I think we should let the men have their coffee and whiskey in the office, don't you, girls? Your pa and Mr Galloway have business to talk over.'

'What *is* your business, Mr Galloway?' Rose asked. 'I'm guessin' you're not a rancher — you don't look leathery and weather-beaten like most of the men in these parts.'

'Why, thank you, young lady,' Thomas said, feigning outrage.

Rose giggled.

'I wouldn't say Will looked leathery or weather-beaten, would you, Ma?' Cora cut in. She turned to Nate. 'Will Hyde's from our neighbouring ranch, Mr Galloway, and he and my sister have an understanding. That's right, isn't it, Rose?'

'Do they indeed,' Nate murmured, and he glanced across the table at Rose.

Rose swallowed her irritation with Cora. 'Cora shouldn't have said that, Mr Galloway. Will Hyde and I don't have an understanding as such. We're good friends, but that's all.'

'Is that so?' he said. 'But to go back to the question you asked, Miss McKinley. I've an interest in the meatpackin' business.'

'Meatpacking!' Rose exclaimed. 'Shouldn't you be in Chicago, then?'

He smiled at her. 'I see you know a bit about the cattle business. The answer is, maybe, maybe not. Sure, the meatpackin' industry's moved west at the same rate as the population's moved west, and Chicago's now fair boomin' thanks to the large-scale meatpackin' houses set up by Armour and Swift. But the West's growin' and developin' at a mighty pace, and there's now talk of building a meatpackin' house south of Chicago. Omaha's been mentioned as a possible town to build one in.'

Thomas nodded. 'I heard talk about that,' he said, 'but I reckon the cattlemen hereabouts won't take to the idea. It'll add to the shipping time for the stock — the longer they're on the railroad, the greater our loss. Havin' a longer drive across the open range, which means less time in a railroad boxcar, is better for the cattle, and that means more money for the cattle owner.'

'But cheapest thing of all is for the ranch owners to slaughter their animals where they're raised and then ship out the dressed meat. It's more expensive to drive live animals across the plains to Kansas City, which is what's happenin' now. By the time they get there, they're fair worn out. And then they've gotta be shipped by rail from Kansas to Chicago. By the time they reach Chicago, many have died in the railcars and most of those that haven't are far too scrawny to fetch much. And that means less money for the cattle owner.'

'All that's true, of course. But you've gotta balance the loss caused by drivin' live cattle and then shippin' them by rail, against the loss caused by shippin' a large amount of dressed beef by rail, and findin' much of it a stinking, rotting mass when it gets to the other end. And that's what happens.'

'That's what *used* to happen, sir.' Nate paused. 'But it won't be happening in the future.'

Thomas straightened up. 'What's your meanin', Galloway?'

'They've finally found a way of sending fresh, chilled beef in ice-cooled railroad boxcars, and they've started successfully shippin' dressed beef from Chicago to New York. You can't get much further east than that.'

Thomas McKinley laughed dismissively. 'I reckon I'd have heard about it now if that was so. Men have been lookin' for ways of shippin' dead beef for years now, but nothing's worked.'

'That was true till this last year, sir.

And then they found the way. Swift and Company got in a man called Andrew Chase. Asked him to design a ventilated boxcar that would keep the beef cool, and he did just that. It's well insulated, with ice packed in a compartment at the top of the car, and meat tightly packed at the bottom to stop it from shifting. And it works, Mr McKinley. It means we can ship our meat as far as we want, so there's no reason not to slaughter the cattle closer to home, at the very moment when the cows are good and fat and will fetch the highest price.

'Well, you don't say,' Thomas said slowly.

'I sure do. You're now gonna see a steady drop in the number of live animals bein' shipped every year, and a rise in the amount of dressed beef being shipped.'

Thomas stared at Nate. 'So what do you want from the ranchers hereabouts?'

'Their help with seeing that Wyoming

doesn't miss out while Omaha booms.'

'And just how can they do that?'

'The railroad runs from the east to the west of Wyoming Territory. There are miles and miles of grass-covered prairie land, stretching out as far as the eye can see. We've got thriving cattle ranches right across the Territory, and they're gettin' bigger and bigger every day as their cows grow fat on Wyoming grass. Why, even Texas cows are driven up to graze on our open range. The way I see it, we should have a meatpackin' house in Wyoming and ship out our own beef. Wyoming cattlemen will benefit; Wyoming Territory will benefit.'

Thomas glanced at Nate, his eyes thoughtful. 'And you say the railroad companies have got these ice-filled boxcars?'

'Nope, not yet, they haven't — but they soon will have. They're holdin' out as long as they can as they've heavily invested in stock cars and animal pens which'll no longer be needed once cattle is shipped out as dressed beef.

But they'll not be able to hold out much longer. The cattlemen won't let them.'

Thomas drummed his fingers on the table. 'You're here for a few days,' he said at last, 'and I know you've already set up a meeting in town on Tuesday where you're gonna be talking to the ranch owners from hereabouts. But when we go into Hope tomorrow, you'll have a chance to meet with some of the neighbours ahead of Tuesday, and I'd sure be interested in hearin' their initial thoughts.'

Nate raised his eyebrows. 'You're talkin' about goin' to church tomorrow?'

Thomas shook his head. 'Nope, we're goin' to a picnic. It's become a local tradition among the people of Hope to celebrate the arrival of summer with a picnic on the edge of town not far from the river. It's a social occasion, of course, and not about doin' business. Here in Wyoming we say that if business is transacted on a Sunday, you'll lose it in the coming week. But

I'm sure it wouldn't go amiss to introduce you to one or two of the ranch owners there.'

'I'd be real grateful, sir.'

Thomas nodded. 'I'll be particularly interested in hearing what Charles Hyde has to say as we're expectin' our two ranches to be workin' closely together in the future, and also Silas Poole. He's a sharp one, but he's got a real nose for what's gonna benefit him.'

Nate nodded. 'I've got his name on my list. I gather he's an important rancher in these parts.'

'He is. But I reckon we'd better leave off talkin' about business — I can see the way my wife is lookin' at me. My last word on the subject is to warn you to keep your eyes peeled when you talk to Silas. He owns a big spread north-west of Hope, but he's not a man who's liked and trusted, for all he's mighty successful. But as I said, we'd better leave any more discussion till tomorrow. I expect the women would rather talk about the clothes they're plannin' on wearing to the picnic than listen to us talkin' about business. Isn't that so, Cora?'

'Why ask me?' Cora retorted sharply. 'Ma and Rose will be wearing clothes, too.'

'Well, that sure is a relief,' her father said cheerfully. 'I wouldn't want our guest to think the ladies in these parts were given to improper behaviour.'

'Pa!' Rose exclaimed. She glanced at her mother's shocked face, and burst out laughing.

Nate grinned at her, then turned to Thomas. 'Perhaps you wouldn't mind if I had a look round the ranch buildings tomorrow mornin' before we leave for town.'

Thomas looked at him, surprised. 'I can't see why not.'

'I used to run a ranch with my brother in the Rock Springs area. That's a few years ago now, but I'd be mighty interested in having a look at how things are done here.'

'I'll show you around,' Rose said

quickly. 'You won't need me, Ma, will you? Everything's done now, isn't it?'

'Jesse will show Mr Galloway round the place, Rose,' Thomas said firmly. 'He'd be better able to answer any questions. You and Cora will both help your ma with packing up the picnic tomorrow morning.' Thomas rose to his feet. 'Now, shall we take up my wife's suggestion and have a whiskey in my office, Galloway?'

'I don't mind if I do, Mr McKinley,' Nate said. He pushed his chair back and stood up.

'Since it looks as if we might be doin' business, and we sure as hell are about to down a whiskey or two together, I reckon you could call me Thomas now, don't you?' Thomas said, moving away from the table.

Cora looked up at Nate, a smile hovering on her lips. But he was staring across the table at Rose. Her smile faded, and she glanced quickly at her sister. Rose was staring back up at Nate, her lips slightly parted.

'If you'll excuse me, ladies,' Nate said, the suddenness of his movement taking them by surprise. He gave them both a slight nod, then turned to Julia. 'Like I said before, Mrs McKinley, that sure was a fine meal, and it's been a real enjoyable evening.' His dark eyes returned fleetingly to Rose, then he turned away from the table and went quickly after Thomas.

Rose stood up. 'You know, I feel real tired now. I think I'll go to bed.' Night, Ma. 'Night, Cora.' She smiled at them both, picked up a kerosene lamp from one of the side tables and went through the dining room to the living area and out into the hall.

'I'm tired, too. Goodnight, Ma,' Cora said. 'If I go quickly, I can use the light from Rose's lamp.' And jumping up, she followed her sister.

Reaching the hall, she saw Rose standing at the foot of the stairs, one hand on the banister, the other holding the lamp, staring towards the door that led to their pa's office. The muffled sounds of men's voices and laughter came from behind the closed door.

Edging back into the living area, Cora moved closer to the panelled wall and stood there motionless, hidden in shadow, watching her sister. She was still standing there when Rose started to make her way slowly up the stairs.

★　★　★

Stepping out from the shadows, Cora felt excitement welling up inside her.

Strong and determined was how Rose had described her earlier that day when they'd gotten back from Hyde Ranch, and as someone who didn't join in as much as she should. Well, Rose should think back to what Ma always used to say when they were little children and Rose would run and complain to her that Cora wouldn't stand up for herself. *Still waters run deep*, Ma would say, and she'd advise Rose never to forget that.

But Rose clearly *had* forgotten it.

Rose had shown her that she'd forgotten it over and over again in the way that she'd kept on ignoring her and Mattie over the years and had never really talked to them. It was as if they weren't worth confiding in, as if they were children who were too young to have womanly feelings or to understand such feelings.

Well, she'd be real surprised to know just how womanly Mattie's feelings for the new cowman were and how much she was hoping he'd soon start courting her. And she'd be even more surprised to know that she, Cora, had feelings for someone, too. And that someone was Will.

Rose didn't deserve Will. She didn't love him in the way Will deserved to be loved. Sure, she was fond of him, but only in the way that Mattie was fond of Will — as a brother. But she clearly didn't feel sisterly about Nate Galloway. Not at all. When had she ever looked at Will in the way she'd looked at Nate? Never. Not so much as once.

Will deserved better than that.

And Mattie thought so, too.

Mattie knew how she'd grown to feel about Will, and she'd often said how hunky-dory it would be if they were sisters, and not just real good friends. And Mattie had also pointed out that no one at either ranch would mind if Will wed Cora and not Rose, as the two ranches would still be united one day and that was the important thing.

Nope, Mattie didn't want Will to wed Rose, who had never been sisterly or even that friendly towards her and Mattie could be counted on to do her best to make sure that Rose never became Mrs Hyde.

Cora's eyes returned to the place at the foot of the stairs where Rose had earlier stood and stared towards the door that hid Mr Galloway from her sight, and a smile flickered across her lips.

It didn't actually look as if much help was going to be needed, she thought in satisfaction. Things seemed to be working out on their own, with Rose having feelings for Mr Galloway that made her go red in the face, and with Mr Galloway having eyes only for Rose. And after the good time she'd had with Will at his ranch that morning, talking and laughing with him before Rose arrived, it was just possible that she was going to end up having the thing she most wanted in life — or rather, the person.

She went slowly across the dimly lit hall to the stairs and gripped the wooden banister rail.

With all of them going into Hope the following day for the picnic, she and Mattie would have the perfect opportunity to start getting her together with Will, and she'd make sure that they made the most of it.

With a gleeful laugh, she ran lightly up the stairs. She couldn't wait for the morning to come.

4

'I'm surprised you're planning on wearing your best dress today,' Cora said, glancing up from lacing Rose into the new white satin corset that her sister had slipped on over her camisole. 'You said you were gonna wear your yellow cotton dress. It's a picnic on the grass, not a wedding or anything like that.'

'I changed my mind. Will likes me in this dress and that's all that matters.'

'Since when have you done anything just because Will likes it?' Cora asked sharply. 'It's always been what Rose wants that matters.'

Rose turned to look at Cora. 'What's wrong with you today, Cora? You've been sounding real funny since yesterday. Have I done something to upset you? Is this still about me comin' early for you yesterday?'

50

'Nothing's the matter,' Cora said lightly. 'I was funnin', that's all.'

'Well, it don't seem funny to me.'

'If you'd turn round and stand still, I could pull your laces tighter.'

Rose stared at Cora's face for a moment, then, her hands on her hips, she turned back to face the mirror.

Cora finished lacing the corset and helped Rose slip her muslin petticoats over her corset, and then her dress on top of them. When she'd done up the tiny pearl buttons at the back of the dress, she stood aside so Rose could see the final effect in the mirror.

'Having a full skirt pulled in at the middle makes my waist look real small,' Rose said, surveying the pale blue lawn dress, covered with small sprigs of white flowers, that dropped to just above her toes. She ran her hand down one of the long smooth sleeves, edged at her wrists with bands of white lace that matched the small piece of lace gathered at her throat. 'Yes, he's gonna like this,' she said in satisfaction.

51

'And which he are you talking about?' Cora asked, meeting Rose's eyes in the mirror.

Rose turned to her, opening her hazel-brown eyes wide. 'Why Will, of course. Who else would I mean?' She glanced down at Cora's green dress. 'You look real nice, Cora. I've always thought green's the best colour for you — it makes your eyes look even greener than they are. You look real pretty.'

Cora blushed. 'You *are* in a good mood today,' she said. 'Any particular reason?'

'Not that I know of,' she said breezily. 'Maybe I'm just grateful that you helped me get into my dress.'

She smiled at Cora, then turned back to the mirror again, leaned forward and arranged her bangs evenly along her forehead. Pulling a few coils out of the hair she'd swept into a pile on top of her head, she let them fall in soft curls around her face, then bit her lips to redden them, pinched some colour into her cheeks and turned to Cora.

'I'll put your hair up for you, and then you must do your lips. You want to look your best, don't you? You never know who'll be there.'

★ ★ ★

Lingering by one of the picnic tables, a glass of lemonade in her hand, Cora watched Will as he stood nearby with his father. Turning her head slightly, she saw Rose on the far side of the picnic area, talking and laughing with Nate Galloway. Looking back at Will, she saw that his eyes, too, kept straying to Rose and Nate, and from the expression on his face, he wasn't too happy about what he was seeing.

She was just wondering whether to ask Mattie to think of a way of getting her pa to go somewhere else so that she could move in and talk to Will, when Charles Hyde was called away to join a group of the neighbouring cattle owners and Will was left on his own.

But he wouldn't be alone for long,

she thought — she wasn't the only woman in Hope who'd like to walk out with Will. From the time he'd developed the kind of looks and the way about him that made a woman feel strange in her stomach, Rose had been the envy of just about everyone in her class.

In fact, Rose seemed to be about the only unmarried woman thereabouts who didn't go weak at the knees when Will stared at her with those blue, blue eyes. She'd never seen Will for what he'd become and she still treated him as a girl would treat her brother. Will would be so much happier with someone else, she was sure, someone who would love him as he should be loved — and that someone was gonna be her.

She turned swiftly to where Mattie was sitting with her ma, and gave her an imperceptible nod. They exchanged quick smiles. Mattie said something to her mother, jumped up, brushed the grass from her skirt with her hand and hurried across to Will before he either moved away or someone else took the place left by his father.

Smiling to herself as she watched Mattie sidle up to Will, Cora strolled over to a place behind them. Idly standing there sipping her lemonade, she surreptitiously strained to hear what Mattie was saying to her brother, while at the same time watching Rose and Nate.

★ ★ ★

'You havin' a good time, Will?' Mattie asked.

He glanced down at her in mild surprise. 'Of course, I am. Why wouldn't I be?'

Mattie shrugged her shoulders. 'No reason.'

Will indicated the people laughing and talking around them, and the trestle tables laden with plates of food. 'It's a mighty fine picnic, and it gets bigger and better every year. We've never had flags and a band before, and we've even got firecrackers this year. Any stranger riding into town today would think they'd got the date wrong and that this was the Fourth of July. What with all the food you womenfolk have made, and being surrounded by friends and neighbours, it'd be hard not to have a good time. So what made you ask, Mattie? And don't say no reason again,' he added dryly.

'I was just wondering.' She paused. 'Have you quarrelled with Rose?' she asked, making sure to keep her tone of voice casual.

He looked at her sharply. 'What makes you ask that?'

She shrugged her shoulders. 'I suppose it's just that whenever I've seen her today, she's been talking to that Mr Galloway — the man staying at McKinley Ranch — and they sure look like they're getting on well.'

He frowned. 'Are you trying to tell me something, Mattie?'

She shook her head. 'Nope. But I

haven't seen you speak to Rose at all today, and with you and her being as close as you are, it seemed a bit funny to me — that's all.'

'There's still a lot of the day left. There's plenty of food waiting to be eaten, and we've not even started the dancing yet, so you can rest your mind — I'll be talking and dancing with Rose before the picnic's over.' He turned slightly to face her. 'But since we're on our own now, I'd like a word with you about something that's starting to bother me.'

'What's that?' Mattie's face was suddenly wary.

'It's the way you've begun to hang around the cowmen, and one cowman in particular.'

'I'm always friendly with the people who work for us. That's how Ma and Pa said we oughta be.'

'You know what I mean,' he said with a wry smile. 'I've seen the way you look at the new ranch hand, and it's what I see in your eyes that worries me.'

'Sam's real easy to talk to,' she said, her voice defensive.

'I'm sure he is. Look, I'm gonna be blunt with you, Mattie. It's not you talking to him I worry about — it's what happens when the talking stops.'

She went red. 'He's just a friend. Aren't I allowed to have any friends? Apart from Cora, that is.'

'He's a hired hand — he'll move on come winter. Don't be forgetting that. He'll be somewhere else next year, and we won't know or care where that somewhere else is. That's the way it is with hired help.'

'You're telling me off for looking at Sam. Are you planning to tell Cora off for looking at you? Not that I mind her looking at you if she wants, though I sure don't know why she'd want to.'

Will stared at her in surprise. He opened his mouth to speak. 'What're you . . . '

'Did I hear my name just now? What are you two talking about, looking so serious?' Cora asked, coming up to them, carrying a plate with some slices of pie on it. 'D'you want a piece of pie, Will?'

Shaking his head, he put his hand on his stomach. 'I couldn't eat another mouthful, Cora, but it was mighty kind of you to think of me.'

She offered the plate to Mattie, who shook her head.

'We were talking about me, Cora,' she said. 'Or rather, Will was doing the talking and I was doing the listening. What's more, he was talking like he thinks I'm still a baby,' Mattie said, glaring at her brother. 'Here, give me the plate of pie and I'll see if anyone wants some — you stay and talk to Will. You're not his sister so he can't speak to you like you're two years old.' She took the plate from Cora, turned abruptly and went over to a group of her friends.

'Don't think we've finished talkin', Mattie, 'cos we haven't,' he called after her, and he turned back to Cora and grinned. 'You'll be sure to stop me if I start talking to you as if you're anything less than your seventeen years, won't you?'

She laughed. 'You can wager I will. Mattie said you were talking about her. Can I ask what about? You can say it's none of my business, if you want,' she added quickly.

'I don't mind telling you. In fact, I think it's something you should be aware of, if you aren't already. In fact, you probably are — you and Mattie are real good friends and I guess you know more about what's in her thoughts than I do. But it's something that's been concerning me.'

Cora screwed up her forehead and looked at him questioningly.

'It's about Sam, the new cowman,' he said. Her forehead cleared. 'It's obvious that Mattie's got a woman's feelings for the man, if you get my drift. I've seen the way she looks at him. She's a real determined gal and can be headstrong, and I'm afear'd for her. Sam's only a hired hand and in the fall, he'll move on. It's what he might leave behind him that worries me.' He glanced quickly at her. 'I guess that's not something I shoulda said in front of a lady. Forgive me, Cora.'

She beamed at him, her eyes shining. 'I can easily forgive you, Will — I reckon that's the first time you've spoken to me as if I'm all grown up.'

'Is that so?' He glanced down the length of her, and she felt a blush start to spread across her chest and up to her face. 'Yup,' he said, with a slow smile. 'It's not just Mattie who's grown up — it's you, too, Cora. You've both turned into beautiful women while I was busy looking somewhere else. I guess that makes me someone who's kinda slow at seeing what's happening right under his nose.' His eyes wandered across the picnic area to Rose, who'd thrown back her head and was laughing at something Nate had said.

'But about Sam,' Cora said quickly. 'Are you gonna fire him?'

Will turned back to her and shook his head. 'It wouldn't be fair on him. He's done nothing wrong and it'd set Mattie against me so bad she'd never speak to me again. All I can do is hope he's an honourable man, who wouldn't take advantage of her feelings for him. But he's never worked for us before and I don't know him, and every time I see her looking at him like she does, it worries me.' He gave her a quick smile. 'But I'm gonna give myself a break from worrying today — Sam's back at the ranch with the animals, and Mattie's here where I can see her.'

'I know what you're saying, Will, and I'll do everything I can to stop Mattie from getting hurt.'

'I'm mighty grateful to you, Cora. You're a good friend to my sister.' He smiled warmly at her. 'But tell me, have you enjoyed the picnic today?'

'Oh, I have,' she said beaming up at him.

'I'm not surprised. Like I said, you're looking real pretty. I wager you'll be standing up for every dance when the music strikes up so I'd better ask you now to save a dance for me or I might miss out. So, will you save me one?'

'Of course, I will,' she said with a laugh. 'Now let's change the subject or I'm gonna go crimson in colour. My red hair's to blame.'

'I don't know about blame — it's a real pretty colour,' he said, smiling into her face. 'But Okay, then — to change the subject, you can tell me about Mr Galloway. He's stirred up a lot of interest around here. Word is that he's looking into setting up a meatpackin' house in Wyoming, but surely that won't happen, not with it being impossible to ship dressed beef any distance without it rotting. I guess it means he'll soon be leaving Wyoming with empty hands.'

'I'm not sure that's so, Will,' she said slowly.

He glanced at her sharply. 'What are you saying?'

'Just that shipping dressed beef's gonna be possible now they've got ice-cold boxcars. The beef won't rot, no matter how far it's shipped. I can see

63

Mr Galloway thinkin' about settling here if things go the way he wants.'

'Is that so?' he said, and he glanced across at Rose. Her head was close to Nate's.

Looking up into Will's face, Cora saw the light dim in his eyes.

'I hadn't realised Rose was so interested in meatpacking,' he said quietly.

5

'You two have been talking together for a long time,' Rose said, coming up to Will and Cora. 'I'm curious to know what you've been saying to each other.' She arched her eyebrow and glanced from one to the other. 'Well, Cora?'

'I'm surprised you noticed anything about anyone else, Rose, you've been talking so much to Mr Galloway,' Cora said with a slight laugh.

'Well, I'm talking to you now,' Rose said airily.

'I guess that's because everyone's finishing eating, and they've started moving around. Mr Galloway's got quite a group about him now, including Pa. No wonder you decided to come back to us.' Cora turned to Will. 'I sure enjoyed talking to you, Will. But if you'll excuse me, I'm gonna go and find Mattie now.'

Will smiled at her. 'Remember, we're gonna have a dance later, grown-up Cora.'

She laughed, gave him a little wave and went off to find Mattie.

Will glanced across at Nate Galloway again. He was deep in conversation with the owners of some of the largest ranches in the area. He turned back to Rose. 'I reckon your Mr Galloway will consider the picnic today a rip-roaring success. I'm guessin' that every cattleman in these parts, no matter the size of their ranch, will be coming to town on Tuesday to hear him speak.'

'He's not my Mr Galloway,' she retorted, 'but I'll let that pass. Are *you* gonna be one of those cattlemen?'

'I sure am. It's an interesting idea, what he's suggesting. Cora's just been giving me a rundown on what he's here for, and Pa's one of those who's talking to him now. We'll certainly wanna hear what he has to say on Tuesday, and we'll be at the general meeting on Wednesday to find out what the mood

66

of the ranchers is. That's when they're all gonna get together to discuss the proposals. I'm also interested in what Silas Poole thinks about the idea. I don't like the man, and I wouldn't trust him any more than I'd trust a snake not to bite, but he's shrewd.'

'I'm amazed Cora was able to remember all the details.' Rose gave a short laugh.

'Don't underestimate your sister,' he said sharply. 'She's a smart gal.'

'I didn't mean to say she wasn't. It's just that it's complicated and we were tired when Mr Galloway was telling us.'

'Not so tired that she didn't take in enough to give me a good idea of what he's here for. And anything she's missed, I'll find out tomorrow.'

'Tomorrow! That's Monday. You mean Tuesday, don't you?' Rose exclaimed. 'I thought Mr Galloway was talking to the townsfolk in two days' time. I'm sure he said Tuesday.'

'He did. You missed hearing your father invite Pa and me to your ranch tomorrow morning to meet with him and Mr Galloway. I think he's gonna suggest that Silas Poole comes, too. It'll be useful for the three of us to have had a talk with Galloway ahead of Tuesday's meeting.'

She looked up at Will in pleasant surprise. 'I didn't know I'd be seeing you so soon again. That'll be nice.' Her eyes strayed back to Nate. 'Talking of Mr Galloway, I think Cora's quite taken with him.' She turned back to Will. 'Don't you agree? Every time I saw her last night, she was watching him closely, and also today.'

'Or she might've been watching you and wondering what you were doing, since you've been with him for most of the day today, and I imagine you were with him for most of yesterday evening,' he remarked dryly. 'He's a good-lookin' man, and he has the way of the world about him. I reckon that would appeal to a woman.' He paused, and glanced at her. '*Does* it appeal?'

Her heart gave a sudden thump.

'What d'you mean?'

'I woulda thought my meaning was clear. You've been so busy talking with Mr Galloway that I've hardly spoken to you today. I've seen more of Cora than I have of you. And like Cora rightly said, you're only here now because the ranchers have finished eating and they're wanting to talk to the man.'

'Yup, he's a fine-looking man and yup, I've talked to him some today. But he's a guest at our ranch and he doesn't know anyone here. And it wasn't so much talking to him as introducing him to our neighbours. That's all there was to it.'

'If you say so,' he said.

'I do say so.' Out of the corner of her eye, she caught sight of a couple of ranchers breaking away from the group around Nate and heading in their direction. 'I reckon those two are planning to join us in a minute. You're right, we've hardly spoken to each other since we got here, and if we don't move now, we're not gonna be able to talk for much longer. Why don't we go for a walk? Just you and me.'

'Okay, if that's what you want,' he said.

She nodded. 'It is. Come on.' She grabbed his hand and they hurried away from the picnic area, heading across the grass-covered slope towards the wooden bridge that spanned the shallow river, which meandered a little way to the side of Hope.

'It sure is a beautiful day,' she ventured as they walked along, breaking into the silence that had fallen between them. She tightened her hold on his hand, gave him a half-smile and then turned away from him and stared across the river towards the rolling green hills. Behind the hills, the bluish-pink mountains rose up to the cerulean sky, their peaks golden in the early afternoon sun.

He glanced at her. 'For someone who had a lot to say earlier today, you're very quiet now, Rose,' he said. 'You suggested taking a walk so we could talk some. But I don't hear much talk coming from you.'

She shook her head. 'It's just I've been thinking.' She could hear the strain in her voice, and she coughed.

'Thinking about what?' he asked after a short pause.

She didn't answer.

'About what, Rose? About your Mr Galloway?'

'Of course not!' She gave a shrill laugh. 'And I told you he wasn't my Mr Galloway.'

'I've known you since we were real little, and I know when something's not right,' he said quietly as they reached the bridge and started to walk across. 'It's not been right all morning, and it's not right now. If you tell me what the problem is, I might be able to help.'

'There isn't a problem,' she said quickly. Then she gave a loud sigh, and stood still. 'I guess that's not true. Maybe there is.' She released his hand and leaned back against the side of the bridge. 'I've been getting so angered with our folks dropping hints every day about you and me. And I know you feel

71

it, too — I've seen you walk away when they start on you. It's why I came to collect Cora yesterday. Ma just couldn't get away from the subject, and I'd had enough.'

'And there I was, thinking you'd come to see me,' he said, a look of feigned surprise on his face.

She gave an awkward laugh. 'That came out all wrong. Of course I wanted to see you, Will. It's just that after listening to Ma all morning — '

' — coming to me was your way of escape.'

'It was more than that. I could've escaped to some place else, if I'd wanted. I could've gone and sat somewhere out of the way, like Jonah's Cabin. I didn't 'cos I wanted to see you. And that's the truth.'

'Okay,' he said, and he smiled at her. His smile didn't quite reach his eyes, she noticed.

'And there was more about the two of us at dinner last night. Pa told Mr Galloway that he and your pa were expecting our two ranches to be working together before too long. And it's not just our folks. Everyone in town looks like they're waiting for us to say something whenever they see us together. The only person who doesn't keep on about us getting wed is Cora. She's been real sisterly and always tries to change the subject of you and me when it comes up. So it's all the hinting that's bothering me, and that's not a problem as such.'

She turned away from him and stared over the side of the bridge at the clear water flowing beneath them.

'I don't think that's the only thing bothering you, Rose,' he said quietly. He put his hand on her shoulder and pulled her gently round to face him. 'Say what it is you really want to say.'

She looked up into his face and met eyes of intense blue, eyes that wanted an answer, insisted on an answer.

'Okay, I will.' Her stomach did a somersault. Struggling to quell her sudden nervousness, she took a deep breath. 'Like you said, we've known each other all our lives. You love me, and I love you. It's not something we've ever said aloud to each other — this is the first time I've said it to you, and you've never said it to me — but it's something we've both known forever. We've never actually talked about us getting wed, though — everyone else is doing that for us. But I was wondering . . . ' Her voice trailed off and she felt herself going red.

'Wondering what?'

'Why you hadn't asked me to marry you.' The words came out in a rush, and she gave an embarrassed laugh. 'I should be real ashamed of myself for asking you that — it's not a thing a lady asks a man. But we know each other so well I feel I can ask it. I'm being really honest with you now, Will — I've been lying awake at night, wondering why you haven't asked me.'

'I reckon that's a fair question. Why don't we go and sit down?'

Her heart missed a beat. 'It's not

a short answer, then.' She attempted another laugh.

He shook his head. 'I guess maybe not.'

He turned away and continued walking across the bridge. Her heart thudding anxiously in her chest, she went quickly after him.

When they reached the other side of the river, he led the way to the trunk of a tree that had toppled over near the water's edge and sat down on it. Rose sat next to him, angling herself to look at him.

'You've been honest with me, Rose, and I'm gonna be honest with you. I've asked myself the same question — why I haven't asked you to marry me,' he said, his eyes fixed on the water.

The air hung heavy between them.

'And what answer have you come up with?' she asked at last.

'I haven't,' he said bluntly.

'I don't understand what you're saying, Will? Are you saying you don't love me?'

He turned to her and shook his head. 'Nope, I'm not saying that. I *do* love you.' A bolt of relief shot through her. 'You were right when you said I loved you,' he went on. 'I always have done, and I always will. And I believe you love me.'

'You're right. I do, Will.' She put her hand on his arm, and felt his lean muscle flex beneath her fingertips.

He nodded. 'The thing that's holding me back is that I'm not sure just how you love me.'

'I don't understand,' she said slowly, taking her hand away.

'You kinda treat me like a brother. That was fine when we were little, but we're older now, and nothing's really changed. I'm not sure if you feel for me in the way a wife should feel for her husband. I've got a sister already — I don't want to find I'm living with another one. I wanna wed a woman who wants me as a man, not as a brother. I'm sorry for speaking blunt like this to you, Rose, but that's the truth of it.'

She coloured. 'Of course I want you like a woman wants a man. But it's not a seemly thing for a lady to talk about.'

'Do you, Rose, 'cos I'm not sure you do. You're right, it's something a respectable woman wouldn't talk about it, but she wouldn't have to. It's not just words can tell a man what a woman feels — it's the way a woman looks at him. I've watched Mattie's face when she's looking at that new ranch hand, and I seen what's in her eyes. I'm scared for her 'cos I see the way she feels about him. I've never seen that longing in your eyes when you look at me. I see a whole lot of liking, but I don't see the thing that'd make your pa come after me with a rifle if he thought I'd acted on it.'

'I promise you, you're wrong,' she cried.

'And what's more,' he went on as if she hadn't spoken. 'I reckon you've asked me that question now 'cos you've met a man who's makin' you feel the way I'm talkin' about, and you're fearful of what that might mean. Suddenly you don't know where you're going, and you wanna feel safe again.'

She shook her head vigorously and stared up into eyes, full of regret and pain. 'You're wrong, Will. Tell me how to prove to you I feel the way a woman should feel about her man,' she said, her voice shaking, 'and I'll do it.'

6

'I mean it, Will,' Rose said quietly, her eyes on the ground in front of her. 'Just tell me what I must do to prove I love you in the way you want.'

There was a moment's silence, then Will burst out laughing. 'You never fail to surprise me, Rose,' he said cheerfully.

She looked at him, puzzled.

Grinning broadly, he jumped down from the tree trunk and held out his hand to her. 'You sure are one amazing woman. But as I can hear the fiddle playing and the sound of dancing, and as I know you love to dance, I'm thinking we oughta let things be at the moment, go back to the picnic and join in the dancing. But only if you think you can rein in this powerful urge for my body that's suddenly come over you.'

She stared at him for a minute, then

she, too, burst out laughing. 'I do love you, Will,' she said, and she took the hand he'd stretched out to her and let him help her down from the log. She tucked her arm into his and they started to walk slowly back to the bridge.

'So nothing's really changed then, has it?' she said. 'We're still best friends, but no more than that. Our folks will have to delay their plans for running the ranches jointly as they're not gonna hear what they want, or not yet at least.'

He glanced curiously at her. 'Listening to you, a person might almost think this was about you being anxious that nothing got in the way of our folks' plans. But I know you, Rose, and I know you don't think like that.'

She smiled at him. 'You're right, I don't. Whatever it was I'd suddenly gotten worried about, it wasn't about linkin' our two ranches.'

They walked along in silence for a few minutes.

'So d'you reckon I could be right

about your feelings for me?' he asked suddenly. 'I know you'd never think of marrying me for the sake of creating a larger ranch, but it's in the fore of our folks' minds, and has been since the time they first saw what good friends we were. Bein' told the advantages of us getting wed and uniting our ranches is something we've grown up with.'

He stopped walking and stared down into her face.

'I want you to think real hard, Rose. I know you've got a brotherly love for me, but like I said, I reckon you've just discovered there are men in the world you could love in a different way. I know I love you in every possible way, but I need you to look into your heart and ask yourself if you would want me for your husband if it weren't for the ranches and everyone's expectations, and even if your answer hurts me real bad, I need you to be honest with me.'

She gazed up at him, and nodded. 'I'll do that. I guess I'm just a bit confused about everything. I've always expected it to be you and me forever, and a part of me has gotten afraid because what's meant by forever hasn't yet begun, and everyone seems to think it should've done.' She positioned her arm more firmly into his, moved closer to him and they started walking again. 'Yup, I reckon that's what it's about, and nothing more than that.'

She sensed him look down at her and she felt the warmth of his affection touch her face.

'Since when have you worried yourself about what everyone thinks?' he said, amusement in his voice. 'That's not the Rose I know. Why, you're much more likely to do the opposite of what everyone wants.'

She giggled. 'How well you know me.'

As they stepped off the bridge at the other side, they heard a dance come to an end, and saw people immediately taking their positions for a square dance.

'Come on, let's not miss the next

dance,' she said, taking hold of Will's hand and starting to run with him across the flattened grass. The first set of couples they reached needed a fourth to complete their square, and they went straight to the empty place next to one of the couples and took up the position opposite the other two. Their hands resting lightly on each other's back, they waited for the music to begin.

Glancing round to see where Cora was, Rose's eyes met Mattie's. She gave Mattie a slight smile. Scowling, Mattie turned away.

She looked at the other couples in Mattie's square and saw that Cora was standing with Nate, her eyes on the ground, waiting for the dance to begin. Cora's hand would be touching Nate's back, she thought, just like hers was touching Will's. She felt a sudden prick of jealousy.

She saw Mattie turn to Cora and say something to her. Cora looked up and met Rose's gaze. For a long moment, her eyes burned into Rose's, and then they moved to Will. Rose saw her sister's expression soften, and her face break into a smile. She glanced quickly at Will — he'd caught Cora's smile and was grinning back at her.

Her heart gave a sudden anxious lurch.

She opened her mouth to speak to Will, but the fiddle and mouth harp sounded the start of the dance, so she turned to face him instead. They bowed to each other, then each took a step closer to the other for the hug that began the dance.

As her arms slid round Will's back, she was suddenly acutely aware of his solidness, of the taut body beneath the thin shirt and waistcoat, of the power in his muscular arms, of the strength in the hands that pulled her tightly to him — the hands that would claim the right to explore every inch of her body once they were wed.

She found she couldn't breathe.

'What say we forget this afternoon, go back to where we were and take things as they come?' he murmured into her ear, seconds before they pulled out of the hug.

Unable to speak, she nodded at him.

They turned to face the centre of the square, held their arms out sideways and linked their hands with the people on either side. As she took Will's hand, a shiver ran through her. But she'd held his hand so many times before, she inwardly cried. Why should she suddenly feel like this, feel so aware of him — more than that, feel so aware of him as a man?

Into her head sprang a picture of herself, naked beneath her nightdress, standing before Will on the night they were wed, waiting for him to come to her, to make her his wife in every way. She shivered again.

As they started to circle to the left, their hands still linked on either side, she wondered whether the shiver had been one of dread or desire.

And what about Cora? Had Cora felt anything for Nate as they'd hugged each other? And if so, what?

She glanced across the dance area to her sister.

Cora was staring at Will. And when all of the circles stopped and the ladies stepped into the centre of their square while the men sashayed to the side, she saw that Cora's eyes were still on Will.

*   *   *

'I do believe it must be my turn to dance with you now, Miss Rose,' Nate said, coming across to her side as soon as the square dance had ended. Cora followed him and stood hovering behind him.

'With your permission, of course,' Nate added, glancing at Will.

'It's Rose's permission you need, not mine, and I reckon she's of a mind to give it to you.'

Rose glanced quickly at Will's face, but it was expressionless.

She turned back to Nate. 'Will reckons correctly, Mr Galloway,' she said lightly. 'I feel quite ready to dance again.'

'In that case . . . ' Nate said. He nodded to Will, took Rose's hand and led her on to the dance area.

The fiddle sounded.

'I guess we've missed this dance, Cora, but perhaps you'll give me the next one,' she heard Will say.

She caught Cora's enthusiastic reply, and then she was too far away from them to hear anything more.

Taking their positions for the dance, Nate's hand resting lightly on her back, Rose found herself facing the place where Will and Cora were standing. They'd moved out of the way of the dancing couples and were engrossed in talking to each other. She felt an acute pang of something she couldn't identify.

Will suddenly looked up in her direction. She gave him a hesitant smile. At the same moment, Nate bent forwards and said something to her. She didn't hear what he'd said as she'd been distracted and not listening properly, but she turned and smiled at Nate in response. When she next looked back at Will, he was once again absorbed in his conversation with Cora, and seemed to have forgotten all about her.

This time, she could identify the emotion that shot through her — it was jealousy.

★ ★ ★

'I sure am lucky that Mr Galloway asked Rose to dance when he did,' Cora said, turning to face Will.

'Why's that?'

'It meant you asked me to dance.'

He glanced at her in amusement. 'But I'd already asked you. I've not forgotten what I said earlier today.'

She laughed dismissively. 'I reckon you would've forgotten. You'd have danced every dance with Rose, if she'd been free.'

He stared at her. 'You're wrong, you

know, Cora. I would've asked you to dance. I've enjoyed talking to you when you've stayed over with Mattie recently, and I enjoyed talking to you this afternoon.'

'Have you really, Will?' Cora beamed up at him.

'I know this is gonna sound plumb crazy, but I kinda feel like I'm starting to see you for the first time. Till not so long ago, you were just Rose's little sister, like Mattie's my little sister, but just as I'm learning I must change the way I look at Mattie now, I'm seeing you with different eyes. Talking to each other like we've been doing, I can see you've grown up.'

'That's real pleasing to me, Will.'

He smiled warmly down at her. Then she saw his eyes drift across to Rose and Nate, who were staring at each other as they danced. Cora followed the direction of his gaze.

She put her hand lightly on his arm, then withdrew it. 'Her feelings for him won't last long, you know, Will. It's just that Mr Galloway's different from everyone around here. He's not a rancher, for a start. He's a business man who's got plans, and his plans take him to towns and places far away. And he's a good-lookin' man with the sort of looks that draw eyes to him, especially a woman's eyes. Being friends with someone like that is new and exciting for Rose.' She gave him a rueful glance. 'But I'm sure her feelings aren't the kind that last — not like her feelings for you — and whatever you say now, when she's seeing clearly again, I'll not be getting the chance to dance with you.'

He looked at her sharply. 'You're saying Rose has feelings for him? I'm not blind — I can see she's bin flirting with him, and he's bin doing the same with her, and I can see she's drawn to him in ways I wish she wasn't — but you're saying she has *real* feelings for him? How can she? She's only just met him. What does she know about the man? What do any of us know about him?' His eyes searched her face for answers, anxiety in their depths.

She put her hand on his arm again. 'I'm sorry, Will,' she said, her voice gentle. 'I shouldn't have put it like that. I don't know what Rose feels, but I'm guessing she'll not feel for him as she feels for you. When Mr Galloway moves on, everything will return to the way it was. You'll see.'

'Will it?' he said slowly, and he turned and stared across the dance area at Rose. 'I wonder.'

Cora glanced up at his profile, and a slight smile of triumph flickered across her lips.

★   ★   ★

With the last signs of the picnic almost cleared away and the dirty dishes packed in the various baskets, ready to be taken back to the wagons, Cora stood with an empty plate in her hands, watching Will, who was standing talking to Rose.

There was a flurry of air at her side,

and she saw that Mattie had come over to her. She gave Mattie a smile and turned back to look at her sister.

'I saw you talking to Will again a while ago,' Mattie said, following the direction of Cora's gaze. 'If he wasn't with Rose today, he was with you. He hardly talked to the menfolk. I reckon my brother's of a mind to take a wife real soon, and I reckon, too, that he's now looking at you, not at Rose.'

'I sure hope so, Mattie,' Cora said, beaming at her. 'You and me, we'd be sisters for real if I wed your brother. But it's not just 'cos I want us to be sisters that I'm looking at Will — I love him and I'd be a good wife to him. You know that, don't you?'

Mattie nodded. 'You'd be much better than Rose. She never thinks of anyone else but herself. I know Will can be a nuisance at times — like he is about Sam at the moment — but everyone says their brothers annoy them, and I reckon he's no worse than any other brother.' She paused. 'To say the truth, he's a real good brother and I want him to be happy.'

'Me, too,' Cora said, and she turned back to look across to Will. 'Me, too,' she repeated under breath. 'And it's me he'll be happiest with.'

7

Rose glanced across to the bed on the other side of the room. The pale light of the moon slanted through the gap in the curtains and fell on the quilt that covered Cora, draining it of all colour. Cora had her back to her so Rose couldn't see her face, but from the sound of her sister's breathing, she was in a deep sleep.

Lucky Cora, she thought, and she stared back up at the ceiling. If only she could close her eyes and fall asleep. But she couldn't. Sleep refused to come as her mind was in too much turmoil. No matter how hard she tried, the things that had happened that day, and the words that had been said, carried on going round and round in her head.

To hear Will say he wasn't sure she wanted him in the way a wife should want a husband had shaken her to the core, and if she was truly honest, it had frightened her. She'd always loved him, and she knew he loved her, and if at any time she'd given any thought to the subject of Will and her and their future together, she'd have decided that everything was just fine between them. But now he was saying it wasn't, and her future suddenly felt less certain. Less safe.

Since he'd said what he had, she'd not been able to stop asking herself if he was right in thinking that, although they loved each other like a brother and sister, theirs might not be the love of a man and wife.

At first, she hadn't completely understood what he was saying. But from the moment she'd slid her hand around Will's back at the start of their first dance together and had felt the hard muscle of his lean body ripple beneath his thin shirt, she'd known what he'd meant.

And looking back to even before that, to the way she'd responded to Nate the first time she'd met him, to the jolt she'd felt run up her arm as her hand had touched his . . .

She'd responded to Nate as a woman might do to a good-looking man. And she'd responded to Will in the same way.

No, she hadn't. She put her hands to her lips and drew a deep breath. She was sure she'd responded to Will in a way that was different, that was deeper. Just thinking about Will now, about the look in his eyes whenever he gazed at her, about the feel of his hard body beneath her fingertips . . .

A powerful shiver ran down her spine and pooled in the pit of her stomach. Then a strange feeling settled deep in her belly, and she felt herself ache low down in a way she'd never ached before.

Wonderingly, she ran her hand slowly across her stomach.

Will had been right, she thought, and she could have burst into tears. He'd always been brotherly Will in her mind, and she'd never once given any thought to him as a man — as the man who was going to bed her; the man who was going to father her children.

But now that she was trying to think about him in a different way, in the way that a wife would . . . Had there ever been a time before that day when Will's touch had made her feel the way that Nate's first touch had made her feel?

She'd often held hands with Will, and they'd frequently walked along in companionship, their arms around each other. Had her heart ever stopped with a sudden longing for more than brotherly friendship from him? As she'd grown older, had she ever felt acutely aware of him, aware of his body close to hers, in the way that she had that afternoon?

If she were honest with herself, no, she hadn't.

She turned on to her side and slid further under the quilt.

Images from long ago when she and Will were children swept into her mind:

how they would abandon their chores, creep out, take their horses and ride away from whichever ranch they were staying in, their rods attached to their saddles; how they would play on the river bank by Jonah's Cabin, fish some, and then throw off all their clothes and swim in the cool water, natural and at ease with each other; how they would spend long afternoons inside the cabin, playing at being a husband and wife having dinner together.

But never venturing into one of the bedrooms in the cabin, she thought. They'd never played in the bedroom. Was there a time, as she'd grown older, when she'd ever regretted that?

Had she ever tried to imagine what it'd be like the first time he stood naked before her as a man, the first time they lay side by side in bed, the first time she felt the touch of his hands on her bare skin, what it would be like when they came together as husband and wife?

Oh Will, she breathed inwardly. Her answer to every question was no.

Then a thought shot into her mind. An ice-cold chill ran through her.

Will had long been of an age to have bedded a woman, and he must have done so. The Will who'd stood tall in the saddle and swirled the lasso high above his head the day before, roping the calf with strength and skill, had been a man, not a boy. How could she have been so blind that she missed the moment when the boy she loved became a man?

There'd never been any woman in his heart but her, she knew. She'd have sensed if there had been, and it was why her parents and the whole town assumed they'd marry. But there were other women in town, women who lived behind the roadhouse — had he visited those women?

A wave of jealousy spread through her. And anger at herself.

Why, oh why, had she never thought about this before?

Silent tears rolled down her cheeks and fell to her pillow. Why had it taken

Will's words, and her response to Nate — a man who was little more than a stranger — to make her open her eyes, question the way she felt, and think seriously for the first time about what she was planning to do?

And what must her folks really think about the two of them?

She rolled on to her back, wiped the tears from her cheeks and stared at the ceiling. If Will had been able to see what was missing from the way she looked at him, their families must surely have seen the same thing, too. Maybe their folks had been so desperately keen on the two ranches working together as one, that they'd been pressing them into announcing their engagement before anything could happen to prevent it.

Like the arrival of a fine-looking stranger.

Will's concern about Mattie had shown her this.

He and his folks could see Mattie's feelings for Sam, so they were keeping a close eye on her and she wasn't going to be allowed to be alone with Sam, if they could help it. But Rose had been alone with Will on countless occasions over the years, even after she'd started her monthlies, and no one had shown any anxiety about them going off together.

And they'd been right not to worry. She tried to remember so much as one occasion in recent months when she and Will had looked at each other, their eyes filled with longing and had struggled to stop themselves from doing anything improper, and she couldn't.

Or had there been such moments, but she'd not noticed them?

Memories crept into her mind of the increasing number of recent occasions when Will had moved closer to her and looked down at her face, his eyes darkening to a deep blue intensity as he'd gazed into hers. Each time though, her mind had been on other things. She'd kept talking and he'd turned away. Why was she only now able to see the yearning that had lain in the depths of his eyes?

How did she truly feel about Will?

When she was little, her ma had given her a cloth doll, which she'd called Martha. She'd taken Martha everywhere with her, even when she no longer played with dolls, as just knowing that Martha was near made her feel safe. Increasingly, as she'd grown older, she'd left Martha at home, knowing that Will had been there to protect her. Had she replaced Martha with Will? Did her feelings for him spring from her desire to feel safe and nothing more?

Was it also possible that the jealousy she felt for Cora — the jealousy she'd have felt towards anyone who grew to have the same closeness with Will as she'd always had — was deceiving her about the way she felt for him?

Or did she genuinely feel something real strong for Will — for what he was, not for what he stood for — something that had been there for a long time, but she just hadn't seen it?

And what about Nate?

It was agonisingly difficult to know what she felt about them both. The first time she'd responded to a man in a way that had hit her body hard had been to Nate, not Will. And at the start of the picnic, she'd chosen to be with Nate. But when she thought back to the beginning of the square dance that afternoon, with Will's words ringing in her ears she'd certainly been conscious of his body in a way she'd never been before, and something deep within her had stirred.

But if she imagined herself touching Nate, imagined Nate touching her, running his hands down the length of her body . . .

She turned on to her other side, her cheeks burning.

What would Cora think of her if she knew the sinful thoughts that were running through her mind?

Cora! Her eyes opened wide. It was only towards the end of the picnic, when she'd realised that Cora and Will were increasingly together, that she'd rather forgotten about Nate in a wave of sudden jealousy.

And now, looking back, when Cora had danced with Nate, he clearly hadn't had the same effect on Cora as he'd had on her that first time she'd touched him. Every time she'd glanced at Cora during the dance, her eyes had been on Will. On Will alone.

Her heart missed a beat.

Until that moment, she hadn't given any thought to the way Cora might feel. But Cora was no longer a child. Should she worry about her sister with Will?

When she'd watched Will at the branding the day before, she'd seen him talking and laughing with Cora and they'd seemed completely at ease with each other. In fact, she'd been a little surprised at how comfortable they were together. Although Cora had known Will all her life, Will had never spent much time with her, always being out with Rose whenever he wasn't helping on his ranch. He'd certainly never been so close to Cora that he'd ever look on her as a sister, and nor would she look on him in a brotherly way.

And now she thought about it, it wasn't just that they'd been talking together — it was the way Cora had been watching Will while Mattie had been watching Sam. Cora's eyes had followed Will everywhere. And then again at the picnic. It was Cora who'd stood at Will's side all the time that Rose was talking and dancing with Nate. And Will hadn't gone over to talk to the menfolk like he usually did — he'd chosen to remain with Cora.

Was it possible that Cora had feelings for Will — the sort of feelings that Will was looking to find in a wife? And could Will be finding he had such feelings for Cora? Was that one of the reasons why he hadn't yet asked her to marry him?

Ice-cold fingers tightened their grip on her heart.

Just as she'd missed seeing Will become a man, she'd missed seeing her sister grow into a woman, a woman that a man could desire. A woman that Will might desire. And who might desire him.

The image of Cora and Will smiling at each other that afternoon filled her mind, and she could see nothing else.

Her body tense, she stared at the ceiling, her eyes wide open, and waited for cold dawn to break.

8

The mid-morning air sang with the murmur of bees and the flutter of the cottonwood leaves that were stirring in the light breeze.

Cora and Mattie rode as near to the river as they could and then slipped down from their saddles. Guiding their horses between the sage-green cotton-woods bordering the river and the silvery gold willows, whose leaf-heavy boughs hung low over the glinting surface of the water, they made their way along the path in the direction of a small cabin that stood back from the water's edge, almost hidden among the trees.

Reaching the stretch of water in front of the cabin, they dropped their reins to the ground and stood back as the horses lowered their mouths and began to drink deeply from the clear water that trickled over and around clusters of pebbles that shone white in the sun.

'They'll be fine for a while,' Cora said, and she turned towards the log cabin and started walking. 'Come on, let's look inside Jonah's Cabin. It's an age since we've been here. I don't know why we stopped coming. We used to come all the time.'

'We grew up, maybe,' Mattie suggested, hurrying after her.

Cora laughed. 'I guess we did.' She paused in front of the cabin and stared at it. 'Maybe we should start coming here again when we want to get away from everyone, like we've done today,' she said, and she went up to the front door made of hand-sawn planks of wood that had been planed smooth, pushed it open and led the way inside.

Walking around the cabin, she opened each of the doors that led from the kitchen-living area to the two bedrooms and store room, and looked inside each room. Then she unbolted the back door and peered up the narrow path leading to the privy. Shutting the door, she slid the iron bolt closed again and turned back into the room.

'It needs a bit of a sweep everywhere, but otherwise it's okay,' she said, throwing herself into one of the two rocking chairs that flanked a large stone fireplace.

'I sure am glad you persuaded your pa to bring you with him today, Mattie,' she went on, rocking her chair backwards and forwards. 'And I'm real glad we decided to come out here — we'd never have been able to talk in private if we'd stayed at the ranch, not with Silas Poole and Mr Galloway there as well.'

'I'm pleased, too. And not just 'cos it's Monday, and anything's better than helping Ma with the washing,' Mattie said with a smile, sitting down in the rocker opposite Cora. She shivered and pulled her shawl tightly around her shoulders. 'Next time we come, we could bring some wood for the potbelly stove. I know it's summer, but it sure is chilly in here.'

'We can easily get wood — there are plenty of trees around here.' Cora glanced around the room. 'I wouldn't want to live here, but I reckon a person could be quite comfortable here for a short time.'

'I guess so.' Mattie paused. 'You said you were wanting to talk, and I'm wondering what you might be wanting to talk about. It wouldn't be my brother, would it?' She looked across at Cora and giggled.

'Maybe, maybe not,' Cora said, a slight blush spreading across her face. 'But since you've started us talking about Will, I was surprised not to see him this morning. I thought he'd come over with you and your pa today as he'd want to talk about Mr Galloway's plans and about the meeting in town tomorrow afternoon, especially as Silas Poole said he'd join them.'

'He was going to come, but the Big Circle horses are arriving today and they're not sure when. Either Will or Pa had to stay at the ranch with Abe to

110

supervise the horses being settled in, and it was decided Pa would come over this morning. I reckon Will would've liked to have come with us today, though,' she added with a knowing smile. 'He seemed real keen on you at the picnic.'

Cora beamed at her friend. 'D'you think so? I sure hope you're right. He's mighty nice.'

'Just nice?' Mattie raised her eyebrows.

'Well, maybe a bit more than that.'

They both giggled.

'What d'you think of Mr Galloway, then?' Mattie asked, rocking her chair again. 'I saw you dancing with him.'

'I don't think about him at all — you know I think about Will all the time. Nope, Rose is welcome to Mr Galloway. She can have him and I'll have Will,' she said firmly.

'And that's what I want, too, and I'm not funning, Cora. You'd be my sister if you wed Will. I'd much rather have you for a sister than stuck-up Rose.'

'That would be perfect. You and me, we're like sisters already, aren't we? You're more of a sister to me than Rose has ever been, and that's the truth.'

'Sure it is. And why shouldn't Will marry you rather than Rose? Like I said before, if you wed Will, it would bring the ranches together, just like him marrying Rose would, and that's all our folks really want, isn't it?' Mattie grinned at her. 'We'll just have to hope it happens.'

Cora stopped rocking, sat forward in her chair and stared at Mattie. 'Maybe we should do more than just hope.'

Mattie frowned slightly. She stared at Cora, and then a nervous smile flickered across her lips. 'What are you thinking?'

Cora sat back. 'I'm thinking we did more than just hope on Saturday that I'd get to talk to Will and that you'd be able to talk to Sam. We planned for me to stay over at your ranch, not to trim the dresses, but to go and watch the boys in the morning, knowing they'd be branding, and hoping we'd have a chance to talk to them, and we did. That was planning, not hoping.'

'That's true.'

'And we didn't just hope at the picnic yesterday — we waited for the right moment and then we struck.' She flicked her wrist sharply in imitation of a snake. 'We planned it so I'd be able to join in your conversation with Will, and then you'd leave. And again it worked.'

Mattie grinned at her. 'It sure did — Will certainly noticed you. I seen the way he looked at you, and he looked real happy when he was dancing with you. D'you wanna come and stay again? Is that it?'

A smile spread across Cora's face. 'I've another idea. Everyone's pushing Will and Rose together, but I reckon we should push Rose and Mr Galloway together.'

Mattie's eyes opened wide. 'You think she's got feelings for Mr Galloway and not Will?'

'I reckon she has. I don't know if she

realises the way she feels about Mr Galloway, but I saw her face when she held his hand that first time they met, and I saw how she looked when they were talking together before the dancing began, and how he looked at her, and I think we should help them see the feelings they have for each other. It'd be a kindness.'

Mattie put her hand to her mouth and bit her lower lip. 'How will we do that?'

'All we've gotta do is get them somewhere by themselves. If we can do that, I'm sure they'll declare their feelings. And when she knows that he feels the same about her — and I'm pretty sure he does — I seen the front of his pants when they were dancing . . . '

'Cora!' Mattie exclaimed.

'Take that look off your face, Mattie Hyde. I'm not saying Rose would act improper — she wouldn't — but the way she feels about him, and the way he feels about her, if we can get them together where they can talk, I'll wager she and Will won't be announcing any engagement.'

'That's easier to say than to do. How would we get them somewhere by themselves? It's Monday now. Our fathers are talking to Mr Galloway and Silas Poole at your ranch right this minute, and we're all gonna have lunch together there when we get back. And with the ranchers' meeting in town tomorrow, Mr Galloway won't have a minute by himself.'

Cora nodded. 'That's true enough.'

'And then on Wednesday the cattle-men are meeting by themselves to chew over what was said at the meeting, and you told me he's gonna go back into town on Thursday to meet up with the ranchers again to hear their thoughts.'

'That's right, so we've gotta act fast. We've gotta come up with a plan before we go back to the ranch this morning — he'll be leaving us on Friday to go to the cattle ranches further away. I know he'll be back in a couple of weeks, but that could be too late — Rose and Will might have announced their wedding by then. Nope, we've gotta come up with a plan right now to get him and Rose alone, and the only day we can get them together is Wednesday. So let's think.'

'Just sitting here thinking is like poking holes in the air with our fingers,' Mattie said a few minutes later, breaking into the heavy silence that had fallen. 'I can't think of anything.'

'Nor me. My mind's empty.'

'We need a place where they can meet, where no one will see them and where they won't be disturbed . . . ' Mattie began. 'What about somewhere in town?'

Cora shook her head. 'It can't be anywhere in town as someone would surely see them there.'

'I guess you're right.'

'What's wrong with us!' Cora exclaimed, sitting upright. 'Why, there's an obvious place for them to meet.'

'There is?'

'Sure.' Cora gestured around her with her hands. 'Here. In Jonah's Cabin. It's far enough from the ranch for no one to come unless they'd got a reason to, but it's easy enough to get here. It's the obvious place.'

A smile spread across Mattie's face. 'You're right. I don't know why I didn't think of it. So all we have to do is come up with a reason to get them both here at the same time. Maybe you can secretly tell Rose tomorrow evening that Mr Galloway wants to meet her here on Wednesday morning, and then tell Mr Galloway the same about Rose.'

Cora vigorously shook her head. 'That wouldn't work. Knowing Rose, she'd go straight to Mr Galloway and ask him why he wanted to meet her at the cabin the next day. She'd never keep quiet about it and then come here alone on Wednesday morning like that, however much she likes him. It'd sound like something improper, and she wouldn't behave like that. Nope, we've got to get 'em here without either knowing the other's coming.'

'How do we do that?'

Cora stared thoughtfully at Mattie. 'You know what,' she said slowly. 'I reckon the answer is Sam.'

'Sam!' Mattie exclaimed in surprise.

Cora nodded. 'Sure. He could pass a message to Mr Galloway after the ranchers' meeting, asking him to come here Wednesday morning. Yeah,' she said, excitement building in her eyes. 'That's what we'll do. And we'll pretend the message comes from Mr Poole. It's the sorta thing Mr Poole would do.'

'And what about Rose? Who'll we ask her to meet?'

'The only person she'd ever come out here alone to meet is Will.' She beamed at Mattie. 'Rose will come here to meet Will, and Mr Galloway will come to meet Silas Poole. But the only people they'll find will be each other.'

'Who's gonna tell Rose that Will wants to meet her?'

'Why, you, Mattie,' Cora said with a laugh.

'What'll I say?' Mattie asked anxiously.

'Just tell her that Will wants to see her somewhere where they can talk undisturbed, I guess. That sort of thing. She'll believe you 'cos she must have noticed that Will's troubled about Mr Galloway. Of course, it means you'll have to come over tomorrow and make sure you bump into Rose when she's by herself. Why don't you tell your ma we wanna do some cooking together?'

'She'd never believe it — she knows we both hate cooking. As it's ironing day tomorrow, she'd only think I was trying to get out of doin' that. And as I've missed helping with the washing today . . . '

'Well, what about saying I urgently need help with a dress I'm making?'

'She's more likely to believe that. She knows how awful you are at sewing. Everyone in town knows you only go to sewing-bees so you can get the others there to do your sewing for you,' Mattie said with a giggle. 'Yup, I'll tell Ma you need my help with some needlework.'

'Come over as soon as you can after breakfast and stay as long as you can. At some point, you'll be able to catch Rose by herself and pass on the message from Will.'

They looked at each other and laughed.

Cora stood up and stretched. 'I guess we oughta go back now,' she said. 'It'll be lunch soon. When we're at lunch, you can say in a real casual way that you've been helping me to cut up pattern-pieces of newspaper in the shape of the dress I'm gonna make. Your pa will be there, and he'll hear that and then he'll back you up when you tell your ma you need to come over here tomorrow.'

'You think of everything, Cora,' Mattie said, her tone of voice admiring. She stood up, and hesitated. 'When Rose and Mr Galloway are together, and you and Will are affianced, you'll help me with my folks and Sam, won't you? I can tell Sam's real keen on me, and I sure am keen on him.'

Cora hugged her. 'Of course I will, Mattie. I wanna see you as happy as I'll be.'

'I hope they're okay about Sam. I'm afear'd that Pa will be real mad with me as Sam doesn't have a spread of his own.'

'But he doesn't have to stay a cowman, does he? Abe's getting real old. Maybe Sam can be your ranch foreman when Abe stops working. That'd make your folks think well of him. Jesse runs just about everything at our ranch, just like Abe does at yours, and you can tell everyone really respects them.'

'They've just gotta keep Sam long enough for him to show them how good he is on a ranch. He's got a real way with the cows, and you should see him breaking in the horses. He used to ride rodeo, that's why. Maybe the Big Circle horses will need breaking in. If they do, I'll ask Will if Sam can do some of them. It's been a mighty good year for us so if Will and Pa see how good Sam is, maybe they'll keep him on over the winter.'

Cora opened the front door. 'So that's decided. Sam's gonna find Mr Galloway after the meeting tomorrow and tell him Silas Poole wants to meet him here on Wednesday morning. You must tell Sam how to get to Jonah's Cabin from McKinley's so he can pass that on to Mr Galloway. You can do that, can't you?'

Mattie nodded. 'Sure thing.'

Cora smiled at her. 'This is the start of making sure we get everything we want. Or rather, everyone we want,' she added with a giggle, and she stepped outside the cabin.

A smile on her face, Mattie followed her and closed the door firmly behind them.

9

'Pass the cornbread, Cora, will you?' Rose asked. As she turned slightly in her chair, her leg touched Nate's and she quickly pulled it back. Nate shifted his position. A moment later, he leaned forward to take the plate of cornbread from Cora and offer it to her, and she felt his muscular thigh against her leg again.

A wave of heat spread through her.

As she accepted a piece of cornbread, she glanced quickly at his face. Raising his eyebrow slightly, he threw her an amused smile, then he turned to pass the plate to her mother, and she was left staring at the sharp angle of his strong jaw.

'Did you want another piece of cornbread, Mr Hyde?' she asked, turning her attention to Will's father, who was sitting on the other side of her.

'Not for me,' Charles Hyde said. 'If I eat any more, I'll break the seat of the wagon the moment I sit on it.' He put his hands on his stomach, looked around the table and laughed.

'I think I'll have another piece after all,' Cora said, leaning across the table to help herself, and smiling at Charles Hyde as she did so. She took a piece for herself and one for Mattie.

Thomas McKinley looked up from his plate. 'You've a mighty fine appetite today, Cora. And you, too, Mattie. What have you two bin doin' all morning?'

'Working hard,' Cora said.

'Doin' what exactly?' her mother asked. 'It certainly wasn't the hard work that comes with helpin' with the washing. You were nowhere to be seen.'

'I've been helping Cora cut the patterns for the dress she's gonna make,' Mattie volunteered. 'We've only just begun cutting them and we've got a heap more to do.'

'I'm mighty pleased to see Cora startin' to take more of an interest in sewing,' Julia remarked. 'It's mending day on Wednesday and there's a pile of darnin' to do.'

Cora laughed. 'Ma likes funning,' she said, smiling across the table at Nate. 'There'd be more holes in the clothes when I finished darning them than when I started.'

He grinned at her. 'My ma wasn't that keen on sewin', either.' He turned to look at Rose. 'What about you, Miss Rose. Is sewing something you like?' he asked, his thigh pressing hard against hers.

She put her hand to her cheeks to cool them down.

'I don't dislike it as much as Cora does. I wouldn't say I'm much better than she is, though.' She felt Cora's eyes on her face, and looked down at her plate.

'Where d'you come from, Mr Galloway?' Cora asked.

He took his eyes from Rose and smiled at Cora. 'From back East originally, but from Rock Springs more recently.'

'Why did you leave the East and come West?' she asked curiously.

'That's surely Mr Galloway's private business, Cora,' Thomas interrupted. 'Ignore my daughter, Galloway.'

'It's fine, sir. I don't mind answering Miss Cora. At a very young age, I packed my bags and came West to help my brother, Ethan, run his ranch. He was already doin' well, but with both of us workin' together, he did even better and we became real wealthy selling beef to the miners in the Rock Springs area. As a result, we were able to build up the cattle operation till we owned more than fifty thousand head of cattle. As we got bigger, I gradually took over more and more of the paperwork, and left Ethan to run the ranch. Before long, we were shipping ten thousand head of cattle annually by rail to the stockyards in Chicago, as well as supplying beef to the miners in all the towns around.'

Thomas gave a low whistle. 'That's a real impressive operation.'

Nate nodded. 'Thank you, sir. I'm real proud of what we achieved. But we did have luck on our side. Rock Springs was the right place to be. With all the mines and timber around Rock Springs, immigrants and fortune seekers were flooding into the area, and the coalmining towns were rapidly swelling in size. The towns needed food, and there we were, able to supply it.'

'Why didn't you stay there, then?' Rose asked.

'In a way I have as I've retained an interest in the ranch. But I'm still young and I couldn't see myself workin' with my brother for the rest of my life. I've too much ambition for that. And also, I reckon there's gonna be big trouble in the Rock Springs area before too long. There are already a large number of Chinamen settled there, and there are more of them comin' in all the time. The mine owners pay the Chinamen less than they pay the whites, so the Chinese miners are gettin' the work. Not surprisingly, the white miners are

127

gettin' pretty mad.'

'That sounds like a real dangerous situation,' Julia McKinley said.

Nate nodded. 'There'll be riots there one day, I'll wager.'

'So how did you get from live cows to dead'uns and meatpacking?' Thomas asked.

'About the time I was startin' to think seriously about gettin' out of the place, I was introduced to some men of business who were interested in seeing a meatpackin' house in Wyoming, and here I am.' He smiled round the table and sat back.

'All this travelling around, I take it you're not wed then, Galloway,' Charles Hyde remarked, leaning slightly in front of Rose to address Nate.

'I've yet to meet the woman who can tame me, sir,' he said with a smile.

Charles and Thomas laughed.

'Well, we're real pleased you decided to bring your ideas to these parts,' Charles told him. 'You've given us plenty to think about. I know I've been givin' it a lotta thought since I met you on Sunday. And I've listened to you this morning and I'll be listenin' real carefully to what you have to say and to the views expressed at the meetin' in town tomorrow.'

'I'm mighty grateful to you, sir.'

'I don't mind tellin' you, the way I'm thinkin' at the moment, I wouldn't wanna see Omaha get any benefits that could've come to Wyoming. After all, we've got the future of our kids to think about.' He smiled warmly at Rose and settled back in his chair.

'I'm inclined to feel in the same way as Charles,' Thomas said. 'But like Charles, I obviously wanna hear what the other ranchers have to say — not just tomorrow, but on Thursday, when they've had time to think about your proposal.'

Nate nodded. 'As you should.' He paused. 'I found it hard to get an inklin' of the way Silas Poole was thinkin' this mornin', and with him bein' so keen to get back to his ranch that he missed a real good lunch, I'm obviously not gonna know for a while longer. For all he doesn't say much, I'm guessin' he's a strong character and could take some of the ranchers with him. Hopefully, he'll take them in my direction,' he added with a smile that took in both Thomas and Charles.

Cora and Mattie exchanged quick glances and then looked down at their plates.

Thomas nodded. 'He's a sharp one, is Silas, but he can be mean with it. And you're correct about his influence in the area. If he decides to support a meatpackin' house here in Wyoming, he'll bring others with him. But you're right that you won't know the way he's thinkin' till Thursday — he always keeps his cards close to his chest. He'll look at the benefit to himself and that'll decide him. Like he said, he'll be at the meeting tomorrow, but I doubt you'll hear him speak. And he'll be at the ranchers' meeting on Wednesday afternoon, but again I doubt he'll speak.

Yup, I'm guessin' it'll be Thursday before you hear his thoughts.'

'I guess I'll just have to be patient,' Nate said.

Charles put his hands flat on the table and started to stand up. 'If you don't think me rude to be leavin' so soon after such a fine meal, Mattie and I will be gettin' off home now. It'll have been a busy day at Hyde Ranch, and a real excitin' one.'

'It'll have been that all right,' Thomas said, smiling at him.

'If we go now, we'll be home before the end of the afternoon, and we might just be in time to catch the horses' arrival. If they haven't already come, that is.' He glanced down at Rose. 'I'm guessin' it won't be long before we see you at Hyde Ranch again, Rose. Will's gonna want to show you the new horses, and I expect you two have got some important plans to make.' He beamed down at her.

She gave him a weak smile and glanced across the table at Cora. Cora raised her eyebrows in a gesture of sympathy.

'I don't know about Rose, but I sure am looking forward to seein' Big Circle horses in action,' Thomas said, standing up. 'I'll try and come over early next week.'

Cora turned quickly to Mattie, who was getting up. 'I won't cut any more patterns till you're there to help me, Mattie,' she said. 'You'll come over tomorrow morning, won't you?'

'If Ma lets me, I will. You mustn't touch the material till I'm with you — you'd be sure to make a mistake.'

'It's very good of you to help Cora, Mattie,' Julia remarked, a trace of amusement in her voice. 'It must be a real upset to you that by doin' so much sewin', you're missin' all your chores this week.'

Mattie and Cora exchanged glances.

'But fortunately, Cora, since you won't be able to do any more pattern-cutting today with Mattie gone,' Julia went on, 'you'll be free to help with the last of the washing. And likely you'll be gettin' back early enough to help your ma, too, Mattie.' She stood up. 'Maybe you could clear the table, Rose. Cora, you'll join Maria and me by the wash tub when you've seen Mattie off.'

* * *

Lengthening purple shadows rolled down the grass-covered slopes as the sun slowly sank behind the darkening hills.

Sitting on one of the sawn-off tree trunks a little way back from the horses' barn, Mattie watched Will as he rubbed down his horse, struggling to conceal her impatience for him to finish the job and move off so she could go into the barn and talk to Sam. She'd seen Sam enter the barn a while before, and as far as she knew, he was still in there.

Having steadily circled the curry brush up from the jaw of his horse, between its eyes, down its neck and shoulders and over its body, Will worked on the inner and outer parts of its legs; then he picked up the stiff brush he'd dropped at his feet and began to brush away the hair and dirt he'd loosened. After that, he carefully combed a tangle of knots out of the horse's mane before giving the horse a brisk rub down with a damp rag.

Mattie felt ready to explode with frustration.

'That's you done, Boy. There's not a single piece of dust left on your coat,' Mattie heard him say at last. 'Now let's give you something to drink and then grain you.'

He straightened up, lightly scratched Boy's nose for a moment or two and then led the horse into the barn. The sound of voices drifted out from inside, and a moment later, Will came out carrying his jacket. Reaching up behind him with his free hand as he walked, he pulled his sweat-darkened shirt away from his damp skin. Catching sight of Mattie sitting there, he dropped his arm and stopped short.

'Hi, Mattie! What are you doin' here?' he asked, going over to her and sitting on the tree stump next to hers.

'I've bin at McKinley Ranch, talking with Cora this morning. We had lunch there and then came home. Then I helped Ma with the washing.'

'Now that's unusual, you helpin' Ma. Usually, you manage to get out of your chores,' he said with a grin. 'So what did you talk about with Cora?'

She shrugged her shoulders. 'Nothing much.' She indicated the barn with her head. 'Are you gonna ride Boy to the meeting in town tomorrow? I thought you said you'd be driving in with Pa.'

'That was the plan, but I changed my mind and decided to ride there. I'm pretty sure Pa will wanna stay on in town after the meeting and talk to the neighbours, and I know I'll be keen to get back to check on the horses, so I've decided to go in on Boy.' He paused, leaned forward and smiled at her. 'Okay, Mattie, what's this really about?

It's not like you to take any interest in what I'm doing. As far as I can tell, you haven't even been out to see the Big Circle horses yet.'

'It's not about anything,' she said quickly. 'Cora told me this morning that she enjoyed talking to you at the picnic. I saw you here with Boy and I came across to tell you that.'

'And I sure enjoyed talking to her, too.' He shook his head. 'But why don't I believe that's the real reason you're here. I guess I must be a mighty suspicious brother, but I kinda get the feeling you've come across to the horses' barn, hoping to see Sam, and not me. Now why would I think a thing like that?'

'I dunno. Why would I wanna see Sam?'

'I reckon you know why,' he said with a smile. He stood up. 'It's time to wash before dinner. Since you came across to give me a message and you've given it to me now, there's no reason for you to hang around here any longer. I'll walk with you back to the house.'

'Actually,' she said, standing up, 'although I didn't come across to see Sam, I might as well have a quick word with him now that I'm here. You go ahead — I won't be a minute.'

'Okay, but I'll wait on the veranda for you. And you'll talk to Sam out here where I can see you.'

She scowled at him. 'I'm not a baby, Will, any more than Cora is.'

'And that's the reason why you'll talk to him out here,' he said firmly, 'and it's why I'll wait where I can see you. I'll go and get him for you.' He went a little way back towards the barn and called for the ranch hand.

Sam appeared at the entrance to the barn. 'Yeah, boss.'

'If you can stop for a moment, my sister wants a word with you.' Will turned back to Mattie. 'A minute, I think you said.' He came towards her, hesitated as he reached her, as if about to say something, then he walked past her and continued across the yard to the ranch house.

Glancing over her shoulder, she watched him sit down on one of the wooden benches in front of the house, settle comfortably into his seat, and pull his cowboy hat low over his eyes. Despite his face being hidden by the brim of his hat, she could feel his gaze on her as he lounged on the bench, staring in her direction.

Turning back to Sam, she gave him a wide smile. 'There's something I wanna ask you to do for me, Sam,' she said.

10

Rose pushed open the front door and stepped out into the cool evening air. Wrapping her crocheted shawl more tightly around her shoulders, she went across to the veranda railing and stared ahead of her at the hills, which stood proud against the night sky — stark black silhouettes on a luminous deep blue expanse that was streaked with gold.

'When night starts to roll over the range, it sure moves quickly in these parts,' a voice behind her murmured.

Startled, she jumped and looked round.

Nate was sitting in a chair to the left of her, his face in shadow, his long legs stretched out in front of him.

'You made me jump,' she said, and she put her hand to her throat. 'I didn't know anyone else was out here. I often come out after dinner and there's never anyone here. I thought everyone had gone up to bed.'

'Well, I guess there are at least two of us who haven't,' he said, taking off his hat and rising to his feet. He dropped his Stetson on to the chair and moved to her side, leaning against the railing next to her. 'At night, I used to stand on the veranda of our house in Rock Springs,' he said, staring ahead into the thickening darkness. 'And there were some nights I'd still be there in the morning. The world feels a mighty big place when you stand alone beneath the stars, but it fills you with a sense of power and you know there's nothing you can't do if you put your mind to it.'

'There aren't any stars tonight,' she said with a nervous laugh. 'And you can sit down again, if you want.' She indicated the chairs behind them.

'I'm real grateful, but I don't want, Miss Rose. And you're wrong about there not being any stars,' he said quietly. Turning to her, he stared deep into her eyes. 'From where I'm standing, I'm almost blinded by stars.

The gold of the sky is shinin' out of your eyes, and it's lightin' up the night.'

She laughed self-consciously. 'Oh, my, Mr Galloway. That doesn't sound like much of a light. I'd better bring out a lamp.'

He shook his head. 'Your eyes are all the light I need.'

'For what?' she asked, her voice strange to her ears, coming as if it was from somewhere far away.

'Why, for what I've wanted to do since the day I met you,' he drawled. 'And for what you've wanted to do since the day you met me.'

'You sure think a lot of yourself,' she retorted lightly. 'But you mustn't talk like that,' she added, pulling her shawl tighter around her. 'It's not proper.'

'Why, Miss Rose,' he said, exaggerated shock in his voice. 'You don't know what I've wanted to do since the day we met. You know only what *you've* wanted to do. Surely you can't be telling me that what you wanna do with me is improper!'

She burst out laughing. 'Since I can't match you for clever words, Mr Galloway,' she said, starting to turn away, 'I'm gonna go inside right now.'

He put his hand lightly on her arm. 'Don't go, Rose,' he said quickly. 'There's no need.'

She looked up into his face, into eyes that were pools of black, and she felt a tremor run through her. 'I think there is, Mr Galloway,' she said, her voice shaking. 'Ma and Pa would be real angry to find me out here alone with you. It's not respectable for a lady to be alone like this with a man she don't know.'

'I seem to remember giving you the story of my life at lunch,' he said with a dry smile. 'So I guess we could say you do know me.'

He raised his hand towards her.

Instinctively, she took a step back. The shawl slipped down her arms.

'Don't be afear'd. I'm not gonna violate you, ma'am,' he said, his voice amused. 'I'm just gonna push a piece of hair back into place. If you'll forgive me.'

He raised his hand to her again, caught up a couple of strands that had fallen from the loose bun into which she'd gathered her long brown hair, and wound them back over her ear. The scent of leather, cigars and maleness embraced her. His fingers lightly brushed her throat and her cheek, and a shiver ran down the length of her spine.

Leaning slightly closer to her as he tucked her hair into her bun, his fingers slipped to the sensitive place behind her ear and lingered there.

Her skin broke out in goosebumps. Low in her stomach, she felt an insistent throb begin.

Catching her breath in a short gasp, she reached out to him, wanting to touch his chest, wanting to feel his hard muscle beneath her fingers. But in a sudden sharp burst of awareness, she swiftly pulled her hand back and stared at him, aghast.

He withdrew his hand from her hair, hooked his thumbs in his belt and took a step back from her. 'You see, Miss

Rose. A gentleman knows how to behave — there was nothing for you to fear. Exceptin' yourself, of course,' he added quietly.

His gaze travelled slowly down the length of her body, and back again to her face. Then his eyes dropped to her lips.

'I'm gonna go in now,' she said.

For a long moment, they stared at each other. Trapped in his hooded gaze, her eyes locked with his, she found she couldn't move.

Silence hung heavily in the air between them.

'Goodnight, Mr Galloway,' she said at last, and she forced herself to turn away and walk steadily into the house.

Closing the door behind her, she leaned back against the cool wood and let out a long, low groan. Had she really been about to touch him like that?

Guilt wound its way through her body.

She struggled to push it back. She'd done nothing wrong and had nothing to feel guilty about. Sure, she'd felt something ache deep in her stomach when he'd touched her face . . . the way he'd touched her . . . But she'd not touched him, not done anything to reproach herself for. She'd walked away from temptation.

Temptation.

She straightened up and felt cold all over. Yes, she'd been tempted by Nate. But a woman expecting to be wed to one man shouldn't be tempted by another, yet she had been. What did this say about her true feelings for Will?

Questions crowded in on her, and she found she couldn't breathe.

The questions frightened her, and she wasn't of a mind to try to answer them. She needed to think, but not that night, not when she was in such a state. She'd ask herself what it all meant the following day. Things were always clearer in the morning.

More urgently, she needed to get out of the hall and into the safety of her bedroom before Nate came back into the house.

She picked up the kerosene lamp from the hall table with one hand, held up her skirts with the other, and made her way up the stairs as fast as she could.

* * *

Lying in the darkness, Cora stared across at Rose's empty bed and listened to the muffled sound of Rose and Nate talking together downstairs outside the house.

They liked each other, she was sure. Much as she hated to admit it to herself, Rose was beautiful. No one in or around Hope came near to matching Rose for the way she looked and the air of niceness that clung to her. It was no wonder that when her sister was around, no one saw her and Mattie. True, Will had started to do so, but deep in her heart she knew it would all change in a moment if Rose looked at Will so much as once in the way she looked at Mr Galloway.

But if Rose were to wed Mr Galloway, and not Will . . .

If only her plan worked!

They wouldn't need long together. With so little time left, Mr Galloway would be certain to make the most of finding himself alone with Rose. Why, he might even propose to her.

She hugged herself in excitement. So much depended upon what happened on Wednesday morning. If it all went well, Wednesday could end with her being wildly happy, and Rose, too.

Of course, if she and Mattie were wrong about Rose being real taken with Mr Galloway . . .

She felt a sharp prick of alarm. She knew she was right about Rose's feelings, but just supposing she wasn't? She needed to think about that.

Hearing Rose's footsteps on the stairs, she turned quickly on to her other side. She was still thinking hard when she closed her eyes and gave in to sleep.

11

The weight of the Tuesday afternoon heat lay heavily on Cora.

Sitting back in the chair on the veranda, she tilted her bonnet forward to shield herself from the bright light and fanned herself while her eyes impatiently scanned the track that led to the ranch.

At last the buggy appeared in the distance, a small speck that grew larger and larger as it neared the house. Before it had even reached the yard, she'd sprung up and moved to the edge of the veranda, and the moment it had passed through the gates, she ran down the steps to greet Mattie.

'Jesse will do the horses,' she called as her friend pulled the buggy to a halt, 'so we can leave them. I told him you were coming and he said he'd look out for you.' She pulled a couple of pails of water over to the horses. 'We'll give them some water and Jesse will do the rest. I can't wait to hear if Sam agreed to say what we wanted.'

'He did,' Mattie said, beaming as she climbed down from her seat. 'I knew he would,' she added, winding the reins over the hitching post. 'He's real helpful like that.'

'He must be. Come on, let's go up and talk.' Cora picked up her skirts and ascended the steps to the house with Mattie close behind.

'I couldn't come earlier as Ma made me do my share of the ironing and then help with the lunch,' Mattie said, following Cora into the living area.

'I guessed that. I'd hoped you'd come this morning, but it doesn't matter — I had chores to do, too. Look, I've already put out some lemonade and flapjacks. We'll be fine in here as there's no one around to disturb us. If anyone does come in, we'll say we're having a break from sewing.' She sat down in one of the deep leather armchairs.

'They won't come in, though. Ma and Maria have finished ironing and are in the vegetable garden now, Pa and Mr Galloway have gone into town for the ranchers' meeting and won't be back till later today, and Rose is resting upstairs. She said she found it hard to get to sleep last night,' Cora added with a giggle. 'I'm thinking it might be something to do with her and Mr Galloway being out on the veranda by themselves after dinner last night. I heard them talking.'

Mattie's eyes opened wide. 'By themselves? Didn't your ma and pa mind?'

Cora shrugged her shoulders. 'They went to bed right after dinner so they didn't know.'

'Will's gone into town, too,' Mattie said, leaning across and taking a flapjack. 'He took Boy rather than go in the wagon with Pa. I asked him real casually what he was doing tomorrow, and he said that he and Pa are coming here tomorrow morning. They all wanna discuss what was said at the meeting today before they go to the ranchers' meeting in the afternoon. I asked if I could come over with them, and Will said I could. I reckon he was mighty pleased I wouldn't be at the ranch alone when Sam was around and he wasn't.'

'Which means they'll want Mr Galloway out of the way tomorrow,' Cora said in satisfaction. 'That'll work out real well. Mr Galloway will know they'll wanna talk among themselves and that he'd do better not to be around, so he'll jump at having a good reason to leave the ranch. He knows he'll find out what everyone thinks on Thursday, and I reckon he'll be real interested in hearing what Mr Poole has to say before that.'

Mattie gave a low whistle of appreciation. 'That's a mighty clever plan, Cora. When he and Rose find themselves alone, they'll be able to talk freely about their feelings for each other.'

Cora nodded. 'And there's one other thing I decided when I was thinking about it all last night,' she said, glancing sideways at Mattie. She took a deep breath. 'I think Will oughta see for himself that Rose and Mr Galloway are meeting each other. All he needs to do is see their horses outside Jonah's Cabin — that'd be enough.'

Mattie gasped. 'It'd make Will real unhappy. D'you think that's necessary?'

Cora nodded. 'Yup, I do. When he finds out they've got feelings for each other, he's gonna be unhappy anyway — there's no way of avoiding that. But if I'm right about Rose, she'll put off telling Will about her and Mr Galloway for as long as possible. I wouldn't even be surprised if she didn't suggest keepin' it a secret till Mr Galloway comes back in two weeks' time. She'd reason it'd be easier for her if Ma and Pa didn't know till then. If she tells them now, less than a week after meeting Mr Galloway, they'd only say it was too soon for her to know her mind.'

'I suppose so,' Mattie said, her voice doubtful.

'When Will knows the truth about

the way Rose feels, he'll be real sad, I know, but I'll be there to comfort him. Then our folks will see Will and me getting on well together and they'll realise it doesn't have to be Rose who marries him.'

'You sure have thought of everything, Cora.' She hesitated. 'Do I have to say something to Will to make him ride out after Rose? I don't know what I could say . . .'

'Nope, he'll be over here so I'll do that. Maybe I'll tell him I heard Rose say she was going to Jonah's Cabin, but I thought she looked real ill when she left. That would be enough to make Will ride out after her. He'd go to help anyone if he thought they might be alone on the range and unwell.' She paused. 'Or I might ask him to help me find my bracelet. I could say I'd lost it somewhere near the cabin when you and I were out there. Yes, maybe I'll say that.' She paused. 'So you reckon that would work?'

'I suppose so,' Mattie said slowly. 'I

guess I feel a mite bad about telling so many lies though, and about how Will's gonna feel.'

'Me, too, and I wouldn't suggest this if I wasn't sure that Rose and Mr Galloway had feelings for each other. But I am, and it can't be wrong to help them just because it helps us, too, can it?'

'I guess not. But just suppose you're mistaken about Rose and Mr Galloway? Will might think he's lost Rose when he hasn't.'

'If I thought for one minute I was wrong, I wouldn't do any of this, even though I like Will a lot. But I noticed them the night they met, the way they looked at each other, and we both saw the way they were at the summer picnic. And then I saw them when they were sitting next to each other at lunch yesterday and again at dinner last night. And when I went to bed, I heard them talking outside the house — just her and Mr Galloway. Rose would never have gone outside alone with him like that if she hadn't got deep feelings for him.'

'No, you're right about that. But even so, she might decide she doesn't want to marry him enough to leave Hope and go and live somewhere far away.'

'That's no reason to marry Will. Will needs someone who really loves him, not someone who's afraid to move away so settles for him,' Cora said sharply. 'And anyway, the way she looks at Mr Galloway, she shouldn't marry Will. He deserves someone who could never look at another man. If Will and I were affianced, I'd never look at anyone else. You know the way I feel about him, Mattie.' She paused. 'You do still want me to wed Will, don't you?'

'Course I do. I'd much rather have you than Rose as a sister.'

Cora nodded. 'I was worried for a minute. And you know I'll help you with Sam when I'm walking out with Will, don't you?' she added. 'Sisters help each other even more than close friends do.'

12

Rose stood in the centre of Jonah's Cabin, her bonnet hanging from her fingers as she stared around the empty room. The windows on either side of the front door creaked beneath the pressure of the wind that was gathering force outside the house.

'Will,' she called tentatively, glancing towards the bedroom doors.

There was no answer.

She put her bonnet on the table and crossed the kitchen-living area to the back door that led outside, and saw that it was still bolted from the inside. He couldn't have gone outside the house through the back door while waiting for her then, she thought, and she turned and went back into the room.

Uncertain what to do, she stood by the table in the centre of the room, biting her lower lip. It was already late in the morning. Could she have missed him because she was late getting there? She hadn't been able to leave the ranch as early as she'd have liked because she'd been forced to do some mending before she went anywhere.

She'd done hardly any chores that week, her ma had complained, and she wasn't getting out of the mending, too. Hopefully it hadn't made her so late that Will had come and gone. Whatever it was he wanted to say to her — and when no one else was around — she needed to hear it.

The clip-clop of a horse's hoofs on hard earth sounded outside.

Relief raced through her — she hadn't missed him after all. She smoothed down her hair and her overskirt, went quickly to the front door and pulled it open.

'Will,' she exclaimed, stepping outside with a smile. Then she stopped abruptly. Nate Galloway was walking towards the cabin, his head bent low against the wind. 'Mr Galloway! What are you doing here?' Her smile died away and she took a step back.

He looked up, saw her in the doorway and stopped. Surprise spread across his face. Frowning slightly, he touched the brim of his hat to her, but she saw that his gaze went over her shoulder to the inside of the cabin.

Then he looked back at her. 'For your sake, I'm sorry it's me here, not Will, Miss Rose,' he said. 'When I rode up, I saw a horse tethered and thought it looked like your mare, but I wasn't real sure.' He went closer to her, his brow creased. 'You asked what I was doin' here. I might ask you the same. It's not that I'm not pleased to see you, 'cos I am. It's just that I'm wonderin' *why* I'm seein' you.'

'I've every right to be here — this has long been McKinley property. I'm expecting Will any time now. You must leave before he gets here.'

'I don't know anything about Will comin' here, but I do know that I'm meetin' Silas Poole here. McKinley property or not, I reckon I'll wait inside if you don't mind. There's a mighty strong wind getting up, and what with the sky takin' on a greenish tinge, and the cattle all lowing and bein' so frolicsome this morning, I'm guessin' there's a violent storm headin' our way.'

'You expected Silas Poole to be here?' she asked in amazement, standing aside to let him go past her into the cabin. 'I don't know why you'd think he'd be here,' she added, following him inside and closing the door behind them. 'Like I said, this is McKinley ground.'

He glanced at her and shrugged his shoulders. 'That's as may be. I reckon I expected Poole 'cos he sent word he'd like to talk with me today and suggested this as a private place I'd be able to find quite easily.'

She shook her head. 'That can't be right. I doubt he's ever been here, and even if he had, he'd never arrange to meet anyone in a McKinley place. Surely meeting in town would have been the easiest thing for both of you.'

'But not as private.'

'Maybe not.' She bit her lip. 'It still seems real strange, though, him asking to meet you out here like this, without anyone else around.'

'Not to me, it doesn't. It's not the first such message I've had from people wanting to see if there's a way of them benefiting more than anyone else. From what your pa has said about Poole, I figured it was very much the sort of thing he'd be after, so I was interested in hearing what he had in mind.' He paused. 'But what made you think that Will would be here at this time of day? Surely he'll be out on the range or workin' at the ranch, especially with the weather not lookin' so good?'

'He sent me a message to meet him here. He said there was something he wanted to talk about without others being around. We used to come here a lot when we were little — it was like our secret hideout — so I wasn't surprised he suggested coming here if he had something he wanted to say in private.'

'Well,' Nate said, taking off his hat, throwing it on the table and looking around the room. 'I don't see any Silas and I don't see any Will.' His gaze returned to Rose's face. 'I see only the two of us.'

Her stomach gave a sudden lurch. 'Do you mind if I look at the note Mr Poole sent you?' she asked hesitantly, and she held out her hand.

'Not at all, but it'd be real hard — it wasn't a written note. His message was given to me by Sam, I think he said his name was. He's one of the Hyde Ranch cowmen.'

'Sam!' she exclaimed. 'Why would Silas Poole give Sam a message for you?'

He gestured bafflement with his hands. 'All I can tell you is Sam came up to me after the ranchers' meeting yesterday just as I was about to get on my horse, and told me that Poole wanted to talk to me in private. He'd suggested I meet him at Jonah's Cabin this morning and Sam told me how to get here. Apparently, Poole hadn't wanted anyone to see him talkin' to me, so he'd asked him to deliver the message.' He paused. 'And what about you — did Will send you a note?'

She slowly shook her head. 'Nope. When Mattie came over yesterday, she told me Will wanted to meet me this morning at Jonah's Cabin. He had something particular to say to me and he didn't want anyone else around.'

He gave her a wry grin. 'You know, I kinda figured you were gonna say something like that.'

They stared at each other.

'If Mattie and Sam were involved in getting both of us here on our own, and they obviously were,' she said at last, 'it means Cora was involved. In fact, Cora will have been behind it. Mattie wouldn't plan anything like this on her own. And nor would Sam.'

'I guess you know your sister and your friends,' he said, pulling out one of the two chairs tucked under the table and sitting down. 'They obviously wanted to get us here by ourselves. Now why would they want to do that, d'you think?' he asked, glancing up at her.

She shrugged her shoulders and sat down on the other chair. 'I've no idea. If I'd known it'd be you here, not Will . . . that it'd be just you and me . . . I wouldn't have come . . . it wouldn't have been right. A respectable lady wouldn't come out to meet a man in a place like this, to be alone with him like this . . . It wouldn't be proper . . . ' Her voice trailed off.

He pulled his chair closer to hers. 'Is that the only reason you wouldn't have come, Rose?' he asked quietly, leaning forward. 'Because you wouldn't want to be seen to be behavin' like one of the fancy women in town? Or is there also another reason?'

A haze of red spread across her chest and up over her face. 'I don't know what you mean,' she said awkwardly, and she cleared her throat.

He straightened up. 'Now why do I

think you do?' he asked with a smile. 'But in case you don't, I'm askin' you to forget about what is and isn't respectable, and answer me honestly. Would you have stayed away if you'd known we were gonna be alone because you don't have the sorta feelings that'd make you wanna be alone with me? Or would you have chosen to come? That's what I'm asking.'

She stared at him, the colour draining from her face. 'I don't know,' she whispered.

He grinned at her. 'D'you want me to help you find out?'

A sudden gust of wind rattled the door, and the windows creaked again.

She jumped up from her chair. 'No, I don't. I'm gonna go now.'

He stood up, crossed to the window in long strides and looked out. 'I'm afraid you're too late — there's a dinger of a storm on the way.' He nodded towards the trees. 'Look at the wind — it's blowin' wild through the cottonwoods.'

She followed him to the window.

Standing behind him, she stared up at the leaden sky. 'I reckon the storm'll be a while yet,' she said. 'I'll get home in time if I leave right now.' She went and picked up her bonnet from the table.

He turned to her, his broad shoulders blocking out the view. 'You won't get back before the storm, which makes that a real bad idea. We'll sit out the storm and then leave. I'll stay at the opposite end of the table,' he added, 'if that'll set your mind at ease. That's if you wanna sit so far from me, Rose. You haven't yet given me an answer to my question.' He took a step closer to her.

Her mouth felt dry.

'You see,' he murmured, his voice caressing her, 'I'm wondering what your sister saw when she looked at us together that made her think she oughta get us alone somewhere. Maybe she sensed there's things we might wanna say to each other, things we might wanna do . . . You know, you're a real beautiful woman . . . '

She gripped her hat tightly, her knuckles white. 'Then she's wrong if she thought that. I'm sure she's wrong.'

'You don't sound too certain to me. *Is* she wrong, Rose?' he asked quietly. 'I'm thinkin' back to the way we've bin together from the moment we met. I'm thinkin' of the look in your eyes when our hands touched. I'm thinkin' that I've seen the same longin' in your eyes that I know's in mine. And I'm thinkin' you ain't too sure any more that it's Will Hyde you want.'

Jet-black eyes searched her face.

Struggling to stop herself from trembling, she took a deep breath.

'I reckon you've been doing too much thinking, Mr Galloway,' she said, her voice shaking.

He took a step closer to her. 'You're right, I've bin doin' too much thinkin' and not enough doing.' She gazed up at him, her eyes opening wide in sudden alarm. 'I reckon it's time I helped you decide what you really want,' he said softly.

Her heart beating fast, she stood motionless, staring up at him.

13

Nate took a step closer to her, and she shivered.

Running his fingers down the side of her cheek and along the line of her jaw, he began to stroke her face slowly, rhythmically, the trace of a smile on his lips. Then with a sudden movement, he cupped her face, lowered his head and brought his mouth hard down on hers.

She gasped inwardly, then her lips started moving beneath his; tentative, exploring.

He pulled her closer still and deepened his kiss, his tongue seeking to open her mouth, and she found herself parting her lips for him. His tongue slid inside her mouth and touched hers.

She jumped back.

Furiously wiping her mouth with her hand, she edged away from him till her back hit the table.

'What am I doing?' she gasped. 'I'm sorry, Mr Galloway. I don't know what came over me. I shouldn't be doing this. I don't want this. Not at all. Not this.'

'Because it's not the way a respectable woman behaves?' he murmured.

'No.' She shook her head vehemently. 'No, that's not the reason. The only man I want like this is Will,' she cried. She stopped and stared at him. 'It's Will I want like this,' she repeated, a sense of wonder in her voice. She covered her face with her hands. 'Why, oh, why didn't I know that till now?'

'Sometimes it takes a stranger to see what lies before your eyes.' His voice was an amused drawl.

She dropped her hands and looked up at him in surprise. 'Did you know I loved Will?'

He grinned at her. 'Put it this way, I was real certain you felt something for Will that you sure didn't feel for me.'

'But . . . '

'But I was different. I rode in from

another world — a world of travelling, of seein' places and doin' business — a world that's a long way from cows and life on a ranch. It wasn't me you were wanting when our hands touched and you went red in the face — it was the thrill of somethin' different, somethin' that seems exciting when you're on a ranch every day from sunup till sundown. I seen it in all the ranches I bin to. It's not me the women are thinkin' about and wantin' — it's what I stand for.'

She stared at him, then broke out into sudden laughter. 'I don't know about lookin' into my heart, but from what I'm seeing when I look at you, Mr Galloway. I reckon you're being a bit hard on yourself.'

'Maybe,' he said, grinning at her. 'But you get my drift. It's a feeling that comes upon a woman real quick, and then it passes. If you look into your heart, you'll see I'm right.'

'What I want to know now is, if you'd been mistaken in your thinking and if

I'd had real feelings for you, and had kissed you back, what would you have done?'

'Well now, Miss Rose,' he said with a lazy smile. 'I'm just a man, and like I said, you're one good-looking woman, so I guess I'd have managed to complete what I started. But that wasn't my intention when I kissed you.'

She smiled at him. 'I'm real glad you did kiss me, though. It showed me what I truly felt.'

'I'm glad to have been of service, ma'am, even though I'm not sure what it says about my kissin', if kissin' me made you realise how much you loved someone else. I guess I'll just have to work on my action.'

They both laughed.

'Whatever it says about your kissing, I'm glad it showed me what I feel about Will.' She paused. 'Will,' she breathed. The colour drained from her cheeks and she stared at Nate in wide-eyed alarm.

'What is it, Rose?'

'Cora's been seeming mighty fond of Will recently. Maybe she didn't just want to get you and me together; maybe she wanted Will to see us together. He and his pa were coming to our ranch today, anyway, to talk with Pa ahead of this afternoon's meeting in town. He and Mr Hyde don't both have to go to the meeting, so maybe she's planned a way of getting Will out here instead.' She shook her head. 'No, she couldn't. She wouldn't do that.'

'You're right, she wouldn't. She'd never be that mean. I reckon this is just about us findin' out what we feel about each other. She'll have seen us together and will have decided we needed to talk somewhere away from the ranch. If she'd wanted Will here, he'd have bin here by now.'

'You're probably right, but if you're not . . . I can't take a chance . . .'

'He wouldn't come now, Rose. Even if she'd planned to send him here, and I think that's unlikely, he'd never have left your ranch when it was clear there was a storm on the way. He'll stay where his help may be needed. There's animals to think about in a storm. They can get real scared in lightning.'

As his words died away, they heard the rumble of distant thunder. The door and windows rattled again.

'It's still far off,' she said, and she hurried to the front door and pulled it open.

Thrown backwards by the strong blast of wind that burst into the room, she staggered back, scarcely able to keep upright. The wind died down, and she dashed again to the doorway and ran outside.

Nate came quickly to her side and caught her arm. 'You can't go anywhere, Rose,' he cried as the wind gusted again. 'The wind's really got up and the sky's darkenin' by the minute. Come back inside — it's gonna rain real hard.'

'Let me go,' she shouted, struggling to free her arm. 'I've gotta get away from here, just in case!'

'Then I'll come with you.'

'No, you won't,' she cried wildly. 'Will mustn't see us together. If Cora thinks I've feelings for you, Will might be thinking that, too. And if he sees us return together . . . '

'You're not listenin' to me, gal. Will won't be goin' anywhere. We're gonna have one almighty cloudburst. It'll mire all the tracks and turn them into rivers of mud within minutes. At least stay here till the storm has passed. I'll put something under the door and we'll keep the water out.'

'I can't stay.' She stopped struggling and stared at him, her eyes panicked. 'We both know there's nothin' happening between us, but if Will finds us together . . . I can't risk him finding me here with you. The ranch is further away from the storm than we are here and Will may already be on the way. He may even be real close by now. I've gotta go.'

A roll of thunder sounded loud above them and a sharp zigzag of lightning split the sky. The neighing of her frightened horse came to her faintly above the booming of the wind. At the same moment, a sudden blast caught Nate's hat. Releasing her arm, he raised his hands to grab at the brim.

She spun round and flung herself across the wind-flattened grass to her horse. Ignoring Nate's frantic shouts, she swiftly unwound the reins from the branch and tugged on them, trying to steady the rearing animal.

With one hand on the reins, she gathered up her skirts as best she could with her other hand, put her foot in the left stirrup and swung her leg over the horse to sit astride in the saddle. Shaking the reins, she bent low over the pommel and spurred the horse forward with her knees.

Just as she reached a gallop, a number of shorts jags of lightning lit up the surroundings with flashes of white fire. There was a loud clap of thunder, and rain began to fall in sheets from the gunmetal sky.

Her head down, she urged her horse

along the path that led away from the river and towards the open grassland and the McKinley ranch. At times slithering on the beaten track that was fast turning into a stream of mud, she galloped as fast as she could through the torrential downpour, her only thoughts being of Will and how soon she could see him and what she urgently had to tell him.

Around her the wind raged, changing direction from one moment to the next, now throwing water into her face, now battering her back with driving rain. But she rode on, gripping the wet saddle as tightly as she could, desperate to widen the distance between her and the cabin.

At last McKinley Ranch took shape through the misty curtain of rain.

Relief coursed through her exhausted body as she saw the fence that surrounded the ranch and the yard. Slowing down, she steered the horse towards the outbuildings and headed for the entrance to the horses' barn. The large wooden door opened as she reached it, and she rode straight through into the dank interior.

'I was calmin' the animals, Miss Rose, when I thought I heard the sound of a horse,' Jesse told her, letting go of the door he'd been holding open and coming across to help her slide her feet out of the wet stirrups and jump down from her horse. He took the reins from her, loosened the cinch and took off the bridle. 'You can leave him with me. When he's drunk his fill, I'll give him some grain and rub him down,' he said, lifting the halter over the horse's neck. 'You get yourself dry.'

She nodded her thanks, started to go out, and then stopped. 'I may go to Hyde Ranch later today if the storm passes early enough to make that possible. But not till I've cleaned myself up, of course. I wanna see if there's been any damage there.'

'I expect Will Hyde will go with you when you do — he'll be keen to check on everything, too. He got here soon after you left. His pa went back when they saw a storm was brewin', which wasn't long after they'd got here, but Will's bin here all morning.'

Her heart leapt.

Pulling her mud-spattered skirts and petticoats up off the wet ground, she turned and half ran from the barn. Sliding at times in the thick layer of wet mud that lay atop the ground, oblivious to the dirt being kicked up on to her sodden clothes by the heels of her boots, she knew only that she had to see Will.

When she got to the foot of the veranda steps, she paused, panting. Having gathered her breath, she walked quickly up to the front door and reached out for the handle, but the door opened suddenly.

Cora stood there. A look of surprise spread across her face. 'You're back,' she said with a slight gasp.

Rose saw her sister glance over her shoulder towards the yard, frown slightly, and then look back at her.

'You're back,' Cora repeated, dejection flattening her voice. 'And you're by yourself.'

'Like you rightly say, I'm by myself,' Rose said quietly. 'I know what you've done, Cora. And I've bin wondering all the way back how my sister could have been behind something that was so unsisterly, and that so shamed herself.'

The blood drained from Cora's face. 'I didn't mean any harm. I thought I was helping.'

'Helping who? You or me? If you look into your heart, I reckon you'll find the answer, and I'm thinking you won't like yourself for it.'

Motionless, they stared at each other.

'Well, it just happens you did help me — you helped me a lot,' Rose said at last. 'So I'm not gonna be mad at you. I reckon you'll be mighty pained if I tell you how much you helped me understand myself, and that can be your punishment. But now I'd like you to stand aside — there's someone I gotta see.'

Cora stared at her, her eyes full of guilt and misery, then she spun round and ran to the stairs. A moment later, she'd reached the landing and the bedroom door slammed shut behind her.

'Rose!' she heard Will exclaim.

Will stood there, filling the doorway with his presence.

'Oh, Will,' she cried, her voice catching in her throat. She took a step forward. 'I'm so glad to see you. I really am.'

He came towards her, staring at her in amazement, then a slow grin spread across his face as he reached her. 'I sure am pleased you feel that way. I'm glad to see you, too, Rose,' he said.

'And you've been here all morning?'

'Yup. I was gonna go back with Pa, but Cora asked me to help her and Mattie find the bracelet Cora lost near Jonah's Cabin on Monday, but in the end the weather made a search impossible. I feel real bad about that. She said it was a favourite bracelet.'

'And you didn't make any attempt to look for the bracelet?'

'Nope. We could see the storm coming, and we knew the tracks would soon be covered in mud and we wouldn't have any chance of finding it. Cora wanted to go, but . . . ' He shrugged his shoulders. 'And talking of mud, Rose,' he said, staring at her in amusement. 'I can hardly see you for dirt — you're covered in the stuff. Cora said you'd gone to town, so why didn't you stay there till the storm had passed? You must have known you were gonna get very wet, coming back when you did. That's not like you at all.'

Suddenly conscious of the way she must look, she put her hand to her head. The pins had long fallen out, she realised; her hair was hanging loose on her shoulders and wet strands were sticking to her damp face. She glanced down at the floor — muddy water was dripping from her clothes and gathering in a pool around her feet.

She looked back up at Will. 'I needed to see you.'

'That sure must have been some

need to get you out in a storm like this.'

'It was,' she said, nodding.

Her heart thudding loudly in her chest, she stood there looking at him, staring at the man she now knew she loved with all her heart and couldn't bear the thought of losing. Fearful of speaking, fearful of what he might say, words wouldn't come.

'Well?' he prompted, and gave her a smile of encouragement.

'I had to tell you, Will.' She gazed up into the clear blue eyes that were looking down at her with affection, the affection she'd always taken for granted. 'I had to tell you,' she repeated.

As he looked down at her, the expression in his eyes deepened into something else, into something she'd seen before, but not understood, not responded to.

'You had to tell me what?' he asked.

She heard him steady his voice, sensed him struggling to push back the hope she could see springing into his eyes.

'That I love you, Will — that I've

always loved you.' Her heart thundered in her chest. 'You were right when you said I loved you as a sister. I have done for most of my life. But at some point that love changed into something else, something much more, something that's given me a powerful ache inside. I was looking in the other direction when that happened and I didn't see it for so long. For far too long. But I see it now, and I know that I will always love you in every way a woman can love a man, and my life will never, ever be complete if you're not at my side for every single day of it.'

'Oh, Rose.' He caught his breath and gazed down at her, a look of sheer joy spreading across his face.

He took a step towards her and held out his arms to her, and she sank into them. As she felt his chin rest lightly on the top of her head, a deep sigh of pleasure escaped her lips. Slipping her arms around his back, she pressed herself as close to him as she possibly could.

'I sure am gettin' wet,' he murmured after a few minutes.

She heard the laughter in his voice and she pulled back. He glanced at the front of his shirt and denims, which were dark with the wetness of rain and mud. Grinning, he raised his hands in a gesture of helplessness, and he looked at her dress. She heard his sharp intake of breath.

Staring down at her clothes, she saw that her soaking wet dress and petticoats had moulded themselves to the curves of her figure like a second skin.

Blood rushed to her cheeks, and she looked back up at him. His eyes caressed her, full of wonder, full of love. Then he dropped his gaze, and she stood motionless beneath the hot touch of his eyes as they travelled the length of her body, then returned to her face.

'Your hair's in a mess from the wind and the rain,' he said, his voice breaking. 'There's mud on your nose, your cheeks and your neck. Your dress is covered in clumps of grass and dirt, but what I see in your eyes — you've never looked more beautiful to me than you look right now.'

'Oh, Will,' she whispered.

'This might not be what a woman would call the perfect moment, but I sure as hell can't wait even as long as it takes for our clothes to dry before I hold you tightly again and ask you to marry me.'

She caught his hands. 'Oh, yes,' she cried. 'Yes, yes, yes.'

His face broke out into an ecstasy of delight and happiness. Beaming down at her, his gaze dropped to her mouth.

Her heart beating fast, she let his hands fall and she stood still, staring up at him, waiting.

Stepping forward, he took her by the arms and pulled her to him. 'I love you, Rose,' he said. 'I always have and I always will.'

She raised her lips to him.

Bending his head towards her, his mouth met hers, and he filled her body with a kiss that went on forever.

We do hope that you have enjoyed reading this large print book.

Did you know that all of our titles are available for purchase?

We publish a wide range of high quality large print books including:
Romances, Mysteries, Classics
General Fiction
Non Fiction and Westerns

Special interest titles available in large print are:
The Little Oxford Dictionary
Music Book, Song Book
Hymn Book, Service Book

Also available from us courtesy of Oxford University Press:
Young Readers' Dictionary
(large print edition)
Young Readers' Thesaurus
(large print edition)

For further information or a free brochure, please contact us at:
Ulverscroft Large Print Books Ltd.,
The Green, Bradgate Road, Anstey,
Leicester, LE7 7FU, England.
Tel: (00 44) 0116 236 4325
Fax: (00 44) 0116 234 0205

Other titles in the
Linford Romance Library:

AN UNUSUAL INHERITANCE

Jean M. Long

Eliza Ellis has a lot on her plate. Although she teaches part-time at the local school, her passion is for baking and cake decoration. When she inherits Lilac Cottage, much to everyone's surprise, she decides to move in rather than sell up. But she also inherits a sitting tenant, in the form of Greg Holt . . . When Eliza gets involved in a new baking enterprise in the village, old memories are stirred up — and Greg knows more than he is telling . . .